I0772594

THE PRESERVE FOR ENCHANTED CREATURES

BOOK ONE - MELLIA

AMANDA MARISOL

ALETHEA INIGUEZ

LIGHTHOUSE CONSULTING

The Preserve for Enchanted Creatures

Book One - Mellia

By Amanda Marisol

ISBN: 979-8-9877791-1-8

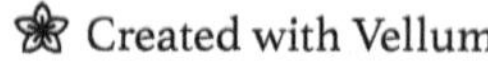 Created with Vellum

To Manikua and Alethea -
"Don't ever let anyone tell you that you can't reach your dreams. Not
even me."
-Pursuit of Happiness, 2006

Loch Ness
Black forest
preserve castle
N

Shiver Breach
Fire Brand
Sanzemble Plains
Cutlery
Aranatorium
The Preserve for Enchanted Creatures
Chaim 2023

PROLOGUE

Gnarled cherry trees formed a tight circle around the glen. Petals scented like vanilla floated down from the dense blanket of soft, white flowers budding on the branches. The air was cool in the glen of Mount Yoshino's summit. The sun cut through the canopy, giving the grove an eerie, pale glow.

Admiral Jonathan Kelgwyn burst into the tight knot of trees, sweating and panting, and realized he was too late. The air smelled of blood.

A troop of wounded, human-sized Satori monkeys sprawled on the ground like abandoned dolls. Several lay with eyes wide open, frozen in terror. Others twitched, barely alive. The admiral recognized the deep slashes and singed fur as a sign of wicked magic, wand blasts meant to kill and maim. The monkeys' bright red blood stained the green moss. In the center of the trees, a large pond shimmered in the sunlight, water turning pink with Satori blood.

Darkentine poachers, the admiral thought to himself, fighting back tears. *I have failed the Guild of Light,* he thought, *but worse, I have failed the Satori.* The poachers killed or incapacitated the adult monkeys, as they could not be trained as telepathic minions. However, they took and raised the babies to use as psychics for their military forces.

The admiral had spent time with many Satori tribes on several of his missions to Japan. He felt grief burst like a bubble of hot oil searing his insides. Through his tears, he saw one of the monkeys move its hand. The admiral leapt into the air, his long white ponytail flying behind him. He landed next to the fallen Satori.

"Alejandra, hurry! Over here!" he called to his wife, forgetting in his panic to use her rank and title of Medic Captain.

He could just hear her tiny footfalls as she sprinted up the trail to the grove. Alejandra was a gnome, and a highly decorated healer for the Guild of Light. This was their third mission together, and both their happy marriage and mission success indicated their admirable team working ability.

Alejandra's long black braids whipped like ropes around her face as she pushed a cherry branch out of her way, breaching the glen. Despite his grief, the admiral admired the way his wife adopted a calculating and unemotional demeanor. Her bright brown eyes took in the horror of the scene, and she pulled out her wand from the inner pocket of her grayish-blue linen tunic.

Crouching over the moribund Satori, she closed her eyes and pursed her lips together, humming a healing song. Waving her smooth oaken wand over the deep cuts in the monkey's forehead, swirls of yellow light flourished around the wound, trying without success to close the bleeding gashes. From her worn, brown leather medical bag, she pulled a silk pouch with a poultice of herbs.

"Jon, put this over the cuts on his head. I think I heard crying just over there."

She tossed the compress up to her husband and ran behind a thick grouping of trees on the outskirts of the grove. The admiral heard Alejandra yell.

"Stop!"

He heard the fear in her voice. With the poultice now sticking to the Satori's wounds, he ran toward the sound of his wife's panicked shout. He drew his wand and a knife from his belt.

The forest was thick and dark outside the glen. Looming pines reached up to the sky, with thick clusters of needles that blocked out the sun. There stood a figure dressed in a black hooded tunic, standing next to a weathered tree. Though he was in shadows, the admiral recognized the stance and sneer of Victor Heatheros, one of the most deadly and infamous wizards in the Darkentine Council.

He was holding Alejandra with one arm by her neck. The toes of her soft cowhide boots almost reached the ground. Her eyes were closed, and her normally tan complexion was turning reddish purple. In his other hand, Victor held his sleek black wand up to Alejandra's face.

"One step closer, and I'll burn her eyes out," Victor threatened. The admiral took a step back. Before he could attempt to negotiate with Heatheros, the poacher waved his wand and disappeared with Alejandra.

The admiral rushed over to where his wife had been a second before. The only signs of her were her fallen wand and the marks where her boots scuffed the dirt near the tree. Dropping to his knees, he put his head in his hands and began to sob. Shaking with pain, the admiral lost track of time.

After what could have been minutes or hours, the admiral heard a weak mewling cry. He saw a black canvas bag next to a fallen log. Something moved feebly inside. Too frail with grief to stand, the admiral crawled over and opened the sack. A minuscule baby monkey stared up at him with the bright lavender eyes common to the Satori. Its white and gray fur was matted with blood, and there was a tiny but deep cut on its chin. He realized the bag belonged to Heatheros, who had abandoned it to take his wife.

With care, the admiral lifted the tiny creature from the bag and held it to his chest. He used the knife to cut the seams of the pouch. He tied it into a makeshift sling and nestled the infant Satori against him. The baby continued to cry softly as the admiral made his way back to the grove, now in the darkness of night.

Raising his wand, the admiral shot a spray of red sparking flares into the sky, signaling for help. He picked up Alejandra's bag, returning multiple cloth bandages, tinctures, and herbs to different pockets. He brushed some dirt off a photograph of himself, Alejandra, and their daughter, Mellia, into his robe pocket, and then began trying to bandage the few monkeys that remained alive.

1

In a swirl of sparks, Mellia winced as the fizz of her body changed from traveling particles to solid form. She felt woozy spellaporting, coming from the moist heat of the Mexican jungle to the wet, chilled, verdant green of the outskirts of Loch Ness.

Before she left, Mellia's grandfather, Sebastian, had packed a satchel with runes, potions, and pouches of herbal remedies they had created together. As he had draped a thick, fur-lined jacket over the shoulders of her thin, embroidered cotton blouse, Mellia had noticed her grandfather's eyes welling with tears. The many-pocketed coat hung limply on her small frame as Sebastian had waved his madrone wand to spellaport his only granddaughter across the world.

She tightened the matted pelt collar and looked around. The Scottish lake spread out before her like miles of glass, smooth and still. In the late, hazy morning sun, a forbidding and bespelled wrought iron gate loomed high, with gnarled, pointed bars reaching like fingers that disappeared in the Scottish mist.

She wished she was fully elfen at that moment, so she could fly over the gate. Being half gnome, she could only leap, and couldn't fly like her father. She wasn't sure she could clear the spiky barbs.

Hanging on the gate was a fancy bronze filigreed sign engraved with the words:

The Preserve for Enchanted Creatures

Master Gamekeeper: Nalina P. Neathersby

A wooden sign hung haphazardly off the side of the Preserve's metal insignia, carved with the words:

Sorceress Extraordinaire

Through the gate, an ancient castle spread out in front of her, looking like an archaic stone lady with windows for eyes and a solid wooden door for a mouth. Moss so green it was almost fluorescent blanketed the walls. Trees with dripping lichen looked like strands of matted gray hair.

Biko, her companion, climbed from inside her coat, and shivered in the frigid weather, nestling in her outer pocket. *I'm cold*, he thought. Biko was Satori, which meant he communicated with the gnelf psychically. The young monkey was entrusted to her by her father, after his family was slaughtered by Darkentine Poachers.

On the left side, perched on the rock wall, was a gargoyle. Mellia couldn't help but notice the stone gargoyle looked awfully lifelike. He had long claws resting on his knobby knees, barbed wings, and a wide, fierce mouth, with a row of pointy teeth. The marble beast had a golden monocle with a chain that dangled over its round belly. The creature's eyes followed her as she approached the gate.

Mellia reached to pull a silver handle dangling from the gate that looked like it would alert someone of her arrival. Then darkness eclipsed the hazy sunlight. Biko became frantic. He pulled on her coat; his eyes wide.

Mellia looked up to see an enormous flying rodent of some kind. Upon closer inspection, the creature had long, slim, white ears with black tips, and white feathered wings that looked borrowed from a wood grouse, but were, in fact, part of the flying creature. The strange rabbit-bird's long, muscular legs pumped powerfully behind his narrow body, all covered in soft gray fur. For an animal that was the size of two adult bears combined, it was moving at a rapid pace. Mellia recognized it as a Swedish Skvader, one of her childhood favorites from *The Duchess Wizard Margaret Cavendish's Guide to Enchanted Creatures.*

As if seeing a giant flying rabbit for the first time wasn't peculiar enough, there was a brown leather harness and saddle flapping in the hare's flight stream. Hanging upside down by his right leg, tangled in a stirrup, was a troll. His face was turning blood-filled beet red. He did not notice Mellia as he failed in his efforts to pull himself up. The rabbit was headed for a thick coppice of trees bordering the clearing of the preserve entrance.

"Dana, stop. Dana, let me down! No more carrots if you don't let me down now!" The troll yelled, his voice deep and melodious despite his clear peril. "Gamekeeper Neathersby will hear about this, Dana. Watch out for the trees!"

Before thinking it through, Mellia leapt as high as she could into the air. "Hold on, Biko!" she yelled as she sailed towards the oversized flying rodent, just grabbing the rabbit's giant left back paw.

Mellia's arms could barely fit around its foot. The rabbit frantically shook its powerful leg, strengthened by a life of bounding and hopping. Mellia held tighter and wrapped her limbs around the rabbit's leg. It raked her with its sharp toenails, tearing at her clothes, just missing her stomach. Feeling the pain, Mellia pushed her legs up, drawing momentum, and hurdled behind its neck so she could ride it like a horse. She pulled the thick scruff of skin, and the rabbit bucked.

"Ahh! That's not helping!" The troll yelled, still hanging from the stirrup.

The behemoth rabbit, troll, gnelf, and monkey were weaving through the forest now, and the troll was swinging towards the rock-hard trunks of silvery birch trees. *Maybe this was a bad idea*, Mellia thought. *Sure was.* Biko answered in his mind.

Mellia couldn't answer the troll's cry; she was holding onto the rabbit's scruff with one hand and pulling up the saddle with the other. In her mind, she was sending the rabbit calming thoughts of fresh grass and a nice warm burrow.

Biko crawled from her pocket, grasping ropes of silken fur and staying close to Mellia in case he slipped. Mellia could feel Biko calming the rabbit with his mind, too, moving one tiny hand onto an area right under its ear. As quickly as the hare had started its furious struggle, its body stilled, except for its wings pumping through the air.

"Climb, Troll!" Mellia cried. Looking over Dana's broadside, she saw the troll exhaustedly pulling himself up, using the rabbit's pelt like handles.

The troll managed to straddle the rodent, settling behind Mellia. He yanked up the saddle, harness, and stirrups, but could not use them during flight. Mellia used the rabbit's scruff to steer it back towards the preserve. It turned through the air.

"Hi. I'm Sollix," the troll said in a cheerful voice, as though they hadn't just subverted disaster while flying on a magic rabbit named Dana.

"Mellia," she replied.

"Right, are you the preserve's new trainee? I heard about you! Admiral Kelgywn's your father--you're famous. His trainings are brutal. I'm still sore from...wait, he came last week. Why didn't you come together?" Sollix asked excitedly.

"That's me," Mellia responded flatly. Sollix grew quiet.

"Did they find your mom?" he asked in a gentle whisper. Mellia clenched her coat closed and gritted her teeth. Biko popped out and shook his head at the troll, placing his tiny index finger to his lips.

After a silence, Sollix sighed dreamily, "Saved by the admiral's daughter. You will have to teach me all of his battle tricks. I actually applied for the Academy of Warriors with my brothers, but I didn't get in," Sollix said, suddenly sounding quiet and sad.

Mellia pretended she didn't hear. Moments later, Sollix shed his sadness as quickly as it had come on, and he replaced it with a giddy excitement. Mellia wasn't sure if he was pretending, if he didn't notice her pensive quiet, or if he was choosing not to care.

"My brothers and I have reenacted all the Guild of Light victories from 'General Wizard Flint Longsword's Battle Accounts,'" Sollix continued.

He began a play-by-play recount of the Russian Battle of Neer. Mellia felt herself enjoying his sing-song tenor and his enthusiasm. As the rabbit descended towards the front of the preserve, Mellia thought, *I'm not here to make friends, I just want to focus on seeing who can help me find my mom.* Biko replied, *you can do both.*

2

Dana landed in the clearing by the gate with a series of gentle hops. Mellia was surprised at how demurely the behemoth hare touched down. An audience had gathered in front of the now-open preserve gate.

Mellia picked out the Head Gamekeeper right away. The cyclops stood around seven feet tall and was clad in a dark brown, creased tweed jacket and skirt, with a white cotton collared shirt underneath. She wore impossibly large leather boots that were laced all the way up to her knees. Her hair was pulled tightly into a twist behind her head, and her fierce, large green eye stared right into Mellia's heart.

Neathersby can see much more than what's in front of her, Mellia mused. *She's way scarier than the admiral.* Biko agreed, *that's a big eye.* He dove into the safety of Mellia's coat.

Neathersby strode over to Dana, and the hare lowered its head to the ground. The Gamekeeper threw the saddle on the penitent rabbit's back. She motioned to a small girl troll who waited by the gate. The troll hurried over, adeptly grasped the reins, and led the rabbit through the gates.

"That's a week with no dessert, Sollix, and a week with no carrots, Dana," Neathersby declared in a clipped Scottish accent.

She turned her focus to Mellia, staring down at the gnelf. Mellia straightened her posture, and stared right back into the cyclops's eye. Mellia found herself almost hypnotized. The green parts of Neathersby's pupil were not just green; swirls of gold and hazel danced around the fist-sized eyeball. The gnelf's hands shook, and sweat beaded on her forehead and upper lip.

"Ms. Mellia Kelgwyn. Welcome to the Preserve for Enchanted Creatures. It's nice to meet you," Neathersby greeted her, shaking Mellia's hand. The cyclops's thick knuckled fist swallowed her thin fingers, and pumped her arm vigorously. Neathersby continued, "I was sorry to hear about your mother."

Before Mellia could respond, Neathersby continued, "It seems your assistance in Sollix's debacle just now was meant to be. He will be your roommate, along with a very respectable Dragon Keeper. Tomorrow, Sollix and Janus will have 30 minutes to give you a tour of the grounds before your shifts. Don't be late."

Neathersby turned on her heel and marched stiffly back into the preserve. *I guess I don't get a thank you for saving the bunny colossus and the troll that won't shut up? Tough crowd,* she thought to herself, relieved that Neathersby had broken her powerful stare. *I think you're brave,* Biko mused from deep in her inner pocket.

3

———————

Mellia felt her stomach knot with excitement as Sollix led the way through the gate, towards a hulking, ancient stone building that would be her quarters. The inside of the castle stretched out before her, a maze of rounded stone arches, mysterious wooden doors, and smooth stone paths. All kinds of beings bustled around in little groups, talking excitedly. Sollix began his tour.

"There's the Magic Market," the troll noted, as he pointed one large, sausagey finger to the left of Mellia.

The center of the castle was a bustling village. With gnomish instinct, Mellia inhaled, smelling the smoke of dragons, wafts of meat pies, and the cloying, flowery perfume of romantic elixirs. Mellia's elfish ears twitched this way and that. She heard gnomes grunting as they dug trenches in lush green garden beds. She heard shop owners shouting about their wares, competing pitches volleying back and forth across a row of rickety wooden stalls. At another station, Mellia could hear the whipping of inky black capes straining like death harbingers, on enchanted strings that bound them to a thick oaken pole.

Pixies leaned forward on outdoor shop counters, waving flirtatiously, batting their eyelashes, seductively selling swirling red bottles of love potions. Mellia watched a gnome pass a beautiful pixie's stand, ignoring her coquettish wink. Mellia flinched as the pixie's dazzling features transformed. Her eyes turned into red slits, and she hissed towards the oblivious gnome, revealing a set of razor-sharp fangs.

"Pixies." Sollix chuckled nervously, as if it was normal for the seemingly benign lady pixie to turn into a growling demon.

Almost forgetting the rabid pixie, Mellia's eyes widened at a stand labeled "Baby Chimera! Touch at your own peril." She could see scaled bodies writhing through the charred metal bars. There were magical ring stands, armor, wands, and other bespelled items.

Mellia was in awe. Her father relied on his superior strength, flight, and ability to read minds. Her mother had stuck with powerful herbal cures and spells. She had never seen so many bespelled things for sale.

"Oh...I almost forgot to tell you about our third roommate, Janus. They should be brushing their hair about now," Sollix explained. As they turned the corner, the stone hallway was dark and lit with torches. Heavy wooden doors with different knockers were spaced evenly down as far as Mellia could see. On Mellia's door, a tarnished bronze griffon hung. Its tail formed the loop of the knocking ring. Sollix pulled the heavy door open with a flourish.

The furniture inside the room was hardly inspiring. There were three plain wooden beds on different sides, with white sheets and cream-colored comforters. A matching steelwood bedside table with an oil lamp, a small dresser, and a desk with a chair were the only other items in Mellia's part of the room.

Sollix had a thick black bear rug on the ground, its mouth open and sharp teeth exposed. He had an ax and a sword hanging on the wall. He also had some sheet music books, which he kicked under his bed. The floor was stone, and a broom leaned against the rock wall corner.

At the back of the room, there was a large mirror with a gold fili-gree frame sitting atop a white vanity table with various potions.

Standing near and looking back at her was the most beautiful person Mellia had ever seen.

Janus's hair was a silky swath that shone an inky black. Light caramel-colored skin glowing, Janus flashed a smile with white square teeth, and the smile traveled up to their narrow eyes, pupils as dark as their hair. A red silk hanfu swirled around Janus, even though there was no wind. The robes were patterned with detailed golden dragons, bewitched to slink across the fabric and wing around the sleeves and front panels.

"I'm Janus Tianshe. Not Miss or Mister, I'm both and neither. So now you know, and you don't have to wonder," they said in a rich, honey-sounding voice. It was neither low nor high, old nor young.

"It's not my business to wonder about it anyway," Mellia said, hiding her admiration of Janus's beauty. *They are beautiful*, Biko thought, now sitting on Mellia's shoulder.

The dragons tittered, backflipping across the red silk of their robe. Janus flipped their hair over their shoulder, "I know." They said. The dragons preened and swirled happily on their fabric. "Well, we're roommates, so you better be clean, and that furry rodent better not smell!"

Mellia's eyes narrowed, and she pursed her lips, "This is Biko, and he's no rodent—he's a Satori from Japan," she growled through clenched teeth. "Be careful—he can tear your mind apart in seconds."

Sensing the growing tension, Sollix interrupted, "Well, it's nearly dinner. Let's head to the banquet hall. Today is cake day!"

"Too bad Neathersby put you off desserts, Troll," Janus countered. In a flash of red and gold swirls, Janus disappeared. Mellia and Biko startled at the bright burst. As if he was used to Janus's dramatic exits, Sollix laughed and motioned towards the door.

4

The Great Dining Hall was a long rectangular building with huge steelwood doors standing open, allowing in the long line of hungry keepers. Mellia saw faces of trolls, pixies, gnomes, cyclopes, and others trudging in, covered in smudges of dirt. They huddled in little groups, chattering and recalling the events of their day. When she crossed the threshold, Mellia couldn't believe her eyes.

The longest steelwood table Mellia had ever seen extended the whole length of the dining hall. It was a flurry of bespelled knives spreading butter on hunks of steaming fresh bread, crystal water pitchers and tea pots filled up glasses and mugs. Fancy filigree gold silverware surrounded stacks of bright white China at each setting. Green napkins folded themselves into swans, knocking forks and spoons into place.

Mellia was wrapped in scents of roasted meats, buttery mashed potatoes, and peppered vegetables. Floating ladles hovered over the food, ready to serve. Biko emerged from the matted fur lining of Mellia's coat. He raised his nose as high as he could, sniffing the aroma heartily. *Mm...cake,* Biko thought at Mellia, and pointed towards the rear corner of the hall.

There stood a dessert tower, overloaded with giant, warm, gooey frosted chocolate cakes piled so high they slid off their trays. Mellia stifled a laugh as Sollix took three pieces and was promptly smacked on the back of the head by a nearby ladle. It wiggled and pointed at him admonishingly. The brownies reappeared back on the tower, and Sollix stared at them longingly.

Mellia looked at Sollix incredulously. At the back of the dining hall, there was a long tunnel oven, with a treadmill contraption running through it. Underneath the treadmill device, a stretch of burning firewood and charcoal heated the whole contraption. Between the dining table and the oven stood a counter with trays full of butter, herbs, spices, onions, celery and carrots.

A tiny hatch opened, and four piglike creatures hopped onto the table. *They are rather graceful for having hooves*, Mellia noticed. The pigs took the butter sticks between their hooves and began rubbing it all over their bodies until they glistened in the low light of the banquet hall.

Mellia heard melodious, joyful humming and realized it was the pigs singing as they sat in the pans on the treadmill, dousing themselves with herbs and spices. The porcine chorus tapered off as the pigs snapped an apple into their mouths, and traversed into the blistering oven.

Mellia felt her stomach twist, realizing the singing pigs would soon be a dinner offering. She settled for mashed potatoes and vegetables, and she found a tray of fish and chips. Biko swiped buttery green beans off her plate with a pickpocket's acumen and speed. He popped the green seeds from their shell, swallowed them without chewing, and threw the husks back on Mellia's plate. She hardly noticed, awestruck at the spectacle of the preserve's mealtime magic.

Feeling less hungry now, Mellia gazed about at the people sitting in tight little groups down the table. At the back, closest to the ovens, a flock of blond-haired pixies were giggling and preening into mirrors they had brought.

"Who brings mirrors to dinner?" Mellia asked sarcastically.

Sollix smiled and motioned with his head towards the ethereal laughter coming from the group. "Those are the pixies and fairies, and they watch over the Glass Vivarium. They may look sweet now, but they can turn mean," he explained.

Sollix motioned to another part of the long table. A group of sturdy-looking, rambunctious trolls and minotaurs tossed bread rolls in the air, using rudimentary magic to transform the rolls into unicorns and pegasus that flew in circles. They pretended they weren't casting longing glances towards the oblivious pixies.

"Some of those are my cousins," Sollix said, looking glum. "They're in charge of the Animals of Extraordinary Sizes, like the Elegons. I wanted to be assigned to the big animals, but I'm not even strong enough to take down a Mandla Lion. I didn't even dare try."

Mellia almost felt sorry for Sollix. His shoulders sagged, but he quickly perked up, remembering his banquet hall tour. "There's the Owltenders," he said, changing the subject.

The Owltenders were a tight group of elves and gnomes, and they all were engrossed in different magical creature guidebooks. The small group of creatures were barely touching their food. They pulled important passages out of their books with their wands, allowing the words to float above the table before they disappeared.

Banquet hall etiquette explained, Sollix dangled a huge pork leg in front of Mellia's nose. It was shiny with fat and dripped butter and herbs, Mellia nearly took a bite of the crispy skin. Then she remembered the smiling pigs humming sweet songs as they glided into the oven. She pushed the pink, greasy limb back towards Sollix.

"Come on, Mellia, live a little. It's delicious," Sollix teased in a sing-song voice.

Janus, who had appeared from nowhere, added, "They are Norse Saerimnir, but we call them Sammies. Neathersby got a whole bunch from Norway a few years back. I heard she won them in a poker match..."

"Gross, I am not eating singing pigs!" Mellia interrupted, punctuating each word with a disgusted tone.

"They are singing because they love to be cooked. After they're cooked, their souls emerge underneath the banquet table of the Viking Demigods in Valhalla, and they eat all of the heavenly scraps that fall to the floor. Then they reincarnate the next day and start all over right here," Janus finished.

Mellia glared at her roommates and slapped extra potatoes on her plate to reinforce her point. Janus looked at her with a frown but said nothing. They had eaten a small bowl of fish and rice that had magically appeared.

About a half an hour later, Mellia and Sollix lumbered out of the dining hall, bellies bulging. Biko groaned loudly from the depths of Mellia's coat and let out an echoing belch. A cold, white fog hugged the castle, covering any sign of stars or the moon.

"It's this way," Sollix said nervously, motioning in the opposite direction Mellia was going.

"I know the way," she snapped, and she began walking towards their room. When she arrived in the room, hoping for some alone time, Janus was already there.

"You should learn to spellaport," Janus advised. Mellia just rolled her eyes and stomped to her side of the room.

5

Laying on her bed, Mellia picked up a leather-bound book with simple gold writing on the front. It had appeared in her room on the dresser while she was eating. She sat down on her bed, surprised at how soft the simple cream-colored mattress felt. Opening the book, entitled, *The Preserve of Enchanted Creatures*, by The Duchess Wizard Margaret Cavendish, she saw a note written by Neathersby had been tucked between the pages. The crisp scarlet ink read,

Dear Ms. Mellia Kelgwyn,

Welcome to the Preserve for Enchanted Creatures. I trust you will find your accommodations suitable.

You have been assigned to the East Asian sector of the park. Specifically, the Satori monkeys. Please read Chapter 7 of the book in its entirety so that you will have full knowledge of caring for these majestic, yet occasionally temperamental, psychic creatures. If you are one of the lucky ones, they will teach you mind control. Otherwise, they will use their power to rip your mind to shreds. They did not prefer their last keeper, and they sent him out of the grove weeping like an infant. He now works with the baby centicore, as they tend to snivel like he does.

I digress, Ms. Kelgwyn. A tip for care--the older Satori love pixie histor-

ical fiction novels. You can find those in the library. Just ask any Owltender. Also, I recommend reading this whole guide, as you may be expected to care for other creatures.

Sincerely,

Head Gamesekeeper Nalina P. Neathersby

Refolding the letter, ropes of sadness coiled in Mellia's gut. She missed her mother, and she was angry that life was moving forward without her. She had given up on her father, wincing upon seeing his name under "Combat Class" on her schedule. Sollix interrupted her thoughts with a particularly loud nasal guffaw, startling her. She did not want to let her guard down, and yet Sollix had been kind to her. A seedling of guilt grew inside of her.

Mellia waited to read the book until Janus went in front of their mirror and brushed their already perfectly swept tresses. Janus looked at her through their gilded mirror, wrinkling their nose, as though Mellia brought rotten fish into their room.

She felt plain next to her glamorous roommate. Her short, shaggy black hair framed her round face. Under her rumpled robes, bruises and cuts patterned her tanned skin. She felt small in the preserve robes, her bony legs and arms swallowed by the thick fabric.

She picked up the guide. With Biko curled up on her shoulder, Mellia flipped to the first page, noticing the animals were listed in alphabetical order. The first entry read:

Amikiri - This dangerous, malevolent creature is the bane of all fishermen near and far. Part snake, part crow, part lobster, this three-foot-long beast tears through the most magic of nets. Ancient relative of the Ikuchi sea monster.

Hunted for their magical gills, which allow the holder to breathe both air and water.

Tricks for caretaking: Bring plenty of sardines, and watch your fingers.

Already intrigued, Mellia turned the page.

Baku - Don't let these cute, tapir-looking fellows fool you. They have the telepathic power to put you to sleep and read your dreams. Using their long nose, they can devour your dreams if they are angry, or your nightmares if they consider you a friend.

Used for dangerous psychic dream reading by the Darkentine Guild.

Tricks for Caretaking: Enjoys croutons and listening to lute music.

With heavy eyes, Biko flipped pages to the letter "S," motioning to a picture of a large white monkey.

Satori- Psychic Japanese simians that reside in the mountains of Japan. These creatures can be benign. They normally communicate peacefully with telepathy and will teach trusted creatures this powerful psychic magic. However, the adult Satori can take over the minds of others, creating a nightmare world of their greatest fears, causing insanity and even death.

Used for mind control by the Darkentine Council.

Enjoy reading historical fiction.

Biko preened proudly, smoothing the hair on the top of his head, and pointing to the page. He smiled with his tiny teeth. Mellia nodded, and patted him on the shoulder.

Mellia began to flip through pages, trying to remember all the tips in the book. The book was packed with information and diagrams, and the colorful pictures swam in front of her eyes as she drifted off to sleep.

6

"Get up!" a now-familiar voice mercifully interrupted the nightmare Mellia was having about her mother. Mellia saw particles of bright light in front of her eyes. Janus was standing across the room, jabbing their wand in Mellia's direction. Sparks were flying towards her and flitting around her field of vision.

"I'm up," she grumbled.

"You're going to be late and miss breakfast," Janus prodded primly.

Mellia waved the lights away from her face as though they were a swarm of flies. She pulled on robes she found in her dresser. Sollix was already gone, and Janus disappeared in their usual flash. By the time she got to the dining hall, the doors were closed.

Sollix and Janus were out front of the large wooden door. Sollix sheepishly handed her a chocolate croissant. Mellia took it grudgingly without thanking him.

Biko came out of her pocket and ripped half of the croissant from her hand, his big purple eyes flashing at her. *Mean*, he thought. He tucked himself back into the warmth of her pocket, and she could hear the monkey chewing his pastry indignantly. Mellia could feel

Janus's eyes drilling into her, but they said nothing. The group headed to the animal sanctuary without talking further.

The zoo was walled in with a thick and sparkling filament fence that extended farther than Mellia could see. A small, yet intimidating goblin sat on a stool. He wore a pointed olive-green captain's hat. He read from a book with a long-haired, muscular elf and a curvy siren on the front. Mellia almost giggled when she realized he was engrossed in an elfen romance novel.

"That's General Fret," Sollix explained. "He guards the gate. He's retired from leading missions." As if on cue, the goblin looked up from his book. He eyed Mellia with his rheumy, piercing gaze.

"Ahh...Mellia Kelgwyn. Daughter of Admiral Jonathan Kelgwyn, our new Combat Class teacher. Late on your first day." He shook his large green head in disapproval.

"You have been assigned to the Satori monkeys. You might think it will be an easy assignment, considering the stowaway in your robe pocket," he said, looking over his glasses at Mellia. "But guard your mind, young gnelf."

Biko lay still, deep in her pocket. Janus and Sollix hurried her through the gate. Mellia shivered. That was the second time in two days an authority figure had cautioned her.

Mellia forgot Fret's warning as she stepped into the zoo proper. A cobblestone path split to the left and right. To the right, a large desert enclosure grew sagebrush and cactus. The terrain reminded Mellia of the time she would leave her jungle villa to gather nahual in the Chihuahua Desert of Mexico. Her heart ached thinking of desert camping trips with her parents and grandfather. They would camp out under the stars and sing songs, sitting shoulder to shoulder to ward off the cold. Grandpa would make his legendary pozole stew.

Sollix interrupted Mellia's memory. She heard him yelling at Dana, the oversized rabbit who had escaped the day before, "You jerk of a flying rodent, you cost me a week's worth of dessert."

The giant creature stared back at Sollix with her large, empty black eyes. Mellia was impressed to see many Skvaders in the pen.

She tried to reach through to pet the rabbit nearest her, and her hand hit a soft, invisible wall.

"That's the Gauze," Sollix said. "It's a powerful spell that keeps the animals inside and safe. We enter through a small steelwood gate."

Mellia rolled her eyes. All magical creatures knew about the Gauze and its important role in separating the magic and human worlds. Ignoring her disdain, Sollix explained that the Gauze stretched all around the preserve, keeping animals safe and poachers out. Mellia noticed a small placard that read "Gravetrail" on the wooden fence.

"You don't want to go into Gravetrail. There's Spikeback Rattlers with stingers on both ends," Sollix said.

From behind a cluster of gray rocks, a lanky keeper rode up on a strange beast that looked like a cross between a horse and a deer. The animal had giant antlers and a short, pointy white tail. It also had muscular, lean legs, hooves, and strong flanks. A tiny wooden sign next to the "Gravetrail" placard read, "Equidae." Mellia figured that was the name of the species before her.

Mellia could not see the face of the stranger riding the Equidae, which was shadowed under a hat that looked like a cross between a conical wizard's hat and a cowboy hat. The stranger pulled back on the creature's reigns, digging their boots into the stirrups. On command, the animal reared up, kicking its hooves towards the Gauze. Though the sharp hooves could not penetrate the magical barrier, Sollix flinched.

"I go on a mission for one lousy week and you almost lose Dana. Am I right, Sollix?" the stranger said teasingly.

"Just like the time my uniceros pinned you, Feign," Sollix retorted.

They tipped their hat up towards Sollix. Mellia's stomach flipped. Feign was their name, mysterious and beautiful. Their skin was a deep chestnut, tanned from being out in the sun. Their deep raven hair was pulled into a loose ponytail that streamed down their back.

Mellia was staring so intently she could see the tiny calluses on Feign's hand and the intricate pattern of stitched swirls on their boots. Sollix noticed Mellia's unblinking gaze towards the shapeshifter.

"You'll want to stay away from Feign, Mellia. They're a shapeshifter," he commented. The gnelf noticed that her roommate was full of strange half warnings.

Mellia felt a jitteriness zipping around her body. It was the sight of Feign, the preserve, and the cryptic warnings she kept getting. She let Sollix pull her to the next section of the Preserve.

7

"That must be the vivarium," Mellia noted, pointing to a giant greenhouse with glass walls, filled with large ferns, monstera, and many plants that she recognized from around her home in Palenque.

Inside the dome, condensation drops clung like diamonds to the glass. Through the fogged glass, Mellia could see fragile, white-winged butterflies fluttering. In a swirl of blond hair and giggles, Mellia recognized the group of pixies that had been sitting at the dining hall. They glided into the dome, waving flirtatiously to Sollix and Janus.

"Mandala, Dewlane, Ashwing, and Enna. Late again, I see," Janus said, flashing their own heart-melting, flirtatious smile. The pixies swooned, and then Mellia noticed the dome doors were made from thick steelwood covered in warning signs. "Do not come near." "Stay back or die." "Deadly." Several skull and crossbones posters were adhered to the door.

"What could Neathersby possibly have put them in charge of?" Mellia asked, voice dripping with disdain.

Always eager to explain, Sollix answered, "We aren't supposed to talk about the endangered animals that we don't directly work with."

"Don't be such a mossback, Sollix. The pixies and fairies watch over the Stinging Lacewings. The Lacewings are enchanting, and they hum the most beautiful tune," Janus said.

Sollix scoffed, "Actually, they are deadly. They lure creatures in with their song and beautiful lacy wings, and then they drive their stinger deep under the skin. Stung creatures will do the bidding of the first being or creature that commands them, but only for three days."

"What happens after three days?" Mellia wondered.

"The victim dies. The venom stops their heart," Sollix said grimly.

"How can that gaggle of cackling pixies manage that level of danger?" Mellia questioned, looking doubtful.

"Pixies are very distantly related to stinging butterflies. They share some of the same makeup. The butterflies don't sting them. In fact, they enjoy the company of the pixies. I saw one of those stingers lick nectar off Enna's hands. In fact, Dewlane went on a mission to retrieve a kaleidoscope of Lacewings from Canada. You can imagine why the Darkentine Council would want these poisonous aviators," Sollix explained.

"Wait...did you say a mission?" Mellia said.

"Well, yeah...so about that," Sollix stuttered.

Janus cut their friend off. "Yes, sometimes as learned experts with animal affinity, we are called by the council to go on missions to save species like the Stinging Lacewing from the Darkentine Council. They hope to use all the stolen and mutilated creatures to strengthen black magic and defeat the Guild of Light. Actually, that's why your father is here. Most keepers need combat training. A lot of combat training." Janus nodded towards Sollix, who was cooing at a dragonfly that had perched on his pinky.

Mellia thought of her mother and the mission to save the Satori monkeys in Japan. She had believed her job at the preserve would be mundane and safe, maybe even kind of fun. Janus and Sollix hinted at a new element of peril.

Ignoring the warning signs, Mellia approached the glass dome and peered through one of the panes. She saw giant white butterflies the size of eagles. Their wings formed intricate lace patterns, helping them effortlessly glide through the air.

She could hear their muffled humming, and it sounded like the song flowers would sing if they could. Mellia felt an intense longing to be near the Lacewings. She inched towards the steel doors, but she felt a firm hand on her shoulder.

"Told you they were enchanting," Janus scolded, pulling Mellia away.

As they walked away from the Lacewing enclosure, Enna's face was pressed against the glass. She hissed with jealousy at seeing Janus walking with Mellia. Her ethereally beautiful features twisted, clear green eyes clouded red, and her benign smile became a row of vicious teeth. Enna watched the duo until she could no longer see them.

Next to the sealed dome loomed the large tree of the Owlery. The owl building was built into a large redwood, which loomed over 100 feet up. Small wooden owl houses and burrows were built into the enormous, fibrous red trunk. Perches for Owltenders hung about the whole tree, joined by braided rope stairs.

Mellia noticed Sollix staring at a handsome Owltender on a lower platform. The boy had curly black hair, wide, doe-like brown eyes, and knobby knees that poked out from under his robes. He had a tawny barn owl perched on his shoulder, and they both read from a thick, brown leather book. Mellia reached for Janus's silken hanfu, trying to quietly point out their friend, the goggling troll.

Janus dodged her and wiggled his fingers, sending a painful magic shock to Mellia's hand.

"Ow!" she cried out. Janus looked at her seriously. "Don't ever touch my robes," he said.

"Ok, that was a snotfondler move of yours to shock me like that," Mellia retorted, her hand and her ego smarting.

"And yes. Sollix has a huge crush on Jayadeva Bhakta, that lovely snack of an elf sitting on that perch. That's one of the dumb reasons, probably the dumbest, that Sollix isn't at the Warriors Academy."

"I think he may have winked at me. Or maybe dander got in his eye," Sollix said wistfully as the trio moved down the path. They walked past a black, windowless building with more warning and danger signs pasted to the doors.

"That's the Arantorium," Sollix informed Mellia. "Endangered and poisonous spiders live in there," Sollix's smooth voice turned high and squeaky.

"Sollix is not a fan of spiders," Janus teased.

"That makes two of us," Mellia agreed.

8

———

They passed what Sollix explained was called the "Sanzembe Plains." Neathersby had cast a Bioweatherus spell, creating a hot and arid ecosystem for the animals. Mellia could see a herd of Elegons flapping their giant, scaly ears. They raised their trunks to the sky and breathed fire from their mouths. They were majestic, looming large in the golden wheat of the meadow.

Trolls dotted the yellow plain, using giant rakes to pick up mammoth piles of excrement. A medium-sized, dark gray Elegon managed to sneak up behind one of the trolls. The Elegon picked him up in the air and tossed him around like a rag doll.

Mellia worried the Elegon had gone mad, but the troll was laughing, even encouraging the creature to launch him higher into the air. The Elegon quivered with joy and smiled a large, fanged grin.

"You should see when they play trolls versus beasts in rugby. Team Elegon has an exceptional strategy," Sollix said.

"It's great that we have a few herds here. Poachers have killed or captured Elegons to near extinction. They take their tusks and use them to carve malevolent ivory wands. They are also great as calvary, as they can fly and are generally destructive."

Mellia didn't think she could hate the Darkentine Council any more, but hearing the grim violence against the animals twisted her insides all over again.

"Next stop, uniceros. That's my station." In another section of the plains, the silver skinned uniceros glimmered under the sun. They lumbered around the field in a tight knot, as though they were fearful of predators. Even though uniceros stood about half the size of the Elegons, with rows of dangerous horns jutting from their noses, the uniceros were equally intimidating.

"They're kind of cute, in a scary way," Mellia said, motioning to a baby uniceros that ran after what Mellia guessed was its mother. "My mom read to me about these guys. They release a silvery ooze that can heal any wound, even those cast by magic. I see why they're here." Sollix looked fondly at his charges. "Yes, they are the sweetest bunch of quadrupeds you could ever know. Molly and Billy over there are the new and proud parents of little Norman, the baby."

"What happened to Molly?" Mellia asked, noticing a pattern of long pink scars striping her wide back.

"Poachers. Fret was on that rescue mission, and he said he got there just in time, seeing as how Molly was pregnant at the time," Janus said grimly.

"Yes, they brought the uniceros here, and then Neathersby asked my parents if I could be a keeper after I didn't get into the Warriors Academy." Sollix said.

"How many times have I offered to train you to fight, troll?" Janus asked, staring at their friend.

"No, it's okay. I'm quite happy here now," Sollix reassured them. "I know this is where I belong. And I couldn't leave little Norman." Hearing his name, the tiny uniceros loped over to the edge of his enclosure. The sides of his wide mouth turned up, as though he was smiling.

The top horn in his growing row of spikes was already large and heavy. The horn whorls looked like polished walnuts stacked on top of each other, narrowing down to a sharp point. They were too big for his head. The uniceros turned sideways and blinked his large, black eye at Sollix.

"Always pet a uniceros from the side," Sollix warned. "Their eyes are on the side of their heads, so they get confused and defensive when approached from the front."

Mellia nodded. Sollix patted Norman's flank and rubbed the sticky goo on a cut on his forearm. The cut transformed into healthy skin. *I'm liking this place more and more,* Mellia thought.

"Where do you work, Janus?" Mellia asked. Janus raised their eyebrows conspiratorially, and smiled mysteriously and smugly at the same time.

Sollix said, "They're in the confidential, high security wing of the preserve, the Fire Brand. They're not allowed to talk about it, or they have to kill you."

Sollix winked at Mellia to show he was joking. Then he added, "No, but seriously, Janus can't talk about it. With their multitude of powers--flight, breathing fire, near immortality, and roasting marshmallows on command--they are the most guarded creature kept from the Darkentine Council."

Janus pointed to a huge black building shaped like a cave. Its wide mouth opened and tapered almost to a point in the rear. The outside was sleek black onyx, and there was a forcefield of some sort surrounding the entire facility. Patches of charred grass bordered the mysterious cavern.

Rather quickly, Janus said, "We will walk you to the Satori, and then we have to check in for duty."

"Next stop, the Satori," Sollix said. "We can finish the tour later--it's time to get to work." Sollix and Janus stopped in front of a thick, blooming cluster of cherry blossom trees. The trunks formed an archway, and past the entrance, the trees were so thick that Mellia couldn't see far. Biko jumped from her pocket and darted into the forest.

"Biko!" Mellia cried.

"It's okay, Mellia. I suspect he's trying to find a relative," Sollix tried to explain. He reached out to grab her, but Mellia had already leapt through the thick arch of blossoms. "They will get in your head!" the troll shouted to the gnelf, but she was already in the glen.

"I guess she will find out the hard way." Janus shrugged and headed towards the Fire Brand. Sollix watched for another minute, worried about his new roommate. Then he realized he was more concerned about further admonishment from Neathersby.

9

After only a short moment inside the grove, Mellia felt a presence in her head. She shook her head back and forth, trying to physically dislodge whatever was invading. *Neathersby's warning*, she thought belatedly. She did not see Biko. Instead, she saw about a dozen large adult Satori slowly and cautiously inching towards her. Several of the monkeys limped, and many had deep purple scars that rose above their fur. *Wand blast scars*, Mellia thought. Their pale amethyst eyes peered into her.

Suddenly, her mind went blank of thoughts. Her head felt as though hundreds of fingers pried it open, somehow viewing her life's memories against her will. She struggled to break the Satori hold, but it only seemed to grow stronger. Her body thrashed to the ground, and she felt the digging into her thoughts like a horrible itch. Her vision went black as the troop lumbered closer.

She woke up covered in cherry blossom petals, as though she had been lying there for days. Her head ached, and at the same time it felt empty, as though someone had scooped the content from her brain.

Looking around, Mellia knew she was not in the same grove as the preserve. There was no archway entrance of cherry trees, and she could smell the sharp, metallic scent of blood nearby. She sat up dizzily, looking around, filled with an anguish as deep as when she lost her mother. The heartache was a physical pain, and it seemed like her chest would split open.

Before her, a dozen Satori monkeys lay on the ground bleeding, most near death. A deep, clear, and brave-sounding voice shouted, and she saw her father enter the grove. With his wand out, he walked right by her, his keen elfen eyes scanning.

"Father, I'm here. I don't know what's happening or where I am," Mellia cried out, now feeling frightened.

The admiral did not acknowledge his daughter. Mellia whimpered a few more pleas, but it soon became clear she was invisible to him. He heard her father call her mother. When Alejandra came into the grove, she looked so beautiful and strong, and she adeptly began healing the savaged simians.

At that moment, Mellia yearned for more time with her mother. She wished she had learned her mother's exceptional healing techniques and embraced her gnome side. She had always just straddled the line between gnome and elf, without connecting to either one.

She watched as her mother heard a cry and ran just out of sight, through a small opening in the trees. She saw a flash, and seconds later she heard her father's sobs. Mellia realized that she was in a forced dream, enchanted by the Satori. She knew they were able to control minds, but she had never known how strong it could be. She knew that her mother would never ignore her in reality.

With that realization, Mellia awoke under the archway back at the preserve. "Why did you show me?" she screamed at the benign group of monkeys.

A voice slipped back into her head, "The truth will heal," it said. At that moment, Mellia realized this group of simians were survivors of the massacre at the grove. Their scars were black magic wounds, from the wand point of Victor Heatheros.

Feeling the twinge of the Satori entering her mind again, Mellia tried to think of a spell to block their telepathy, but suddenly she felt soothed. Her body warmed. Her muscles relaxed, and her mind was peaceful. She felt the sharp edge of anger towards her father blunt, but not disappear.

After seeing the horrific scene unfold, she still believed her mother could have been saved somehow. At that moment, one of the large monkeys produced a frantic, tiny Biko from behind her back. The little monkey scampered over to his guardian, purple eyes wide with concern.

"I'm okay, Biko. Just a little headache is all," she explained.

The Satori beckoned Mellia into their seated circle and made a place for her. For the rest of the day, the psychic monkeys squatted, crowding her and telling stories with their minds. This group of Satori had been saved from the Darkentine poachers but much grieved their other fallen kin. They knew that some of their clan had been turned into Darkentine army psychics because their telepathic ties had been cut with dark magic. The gnelf and the preserve Satori bonded over their mutual grief.

They understood Mellia had lost her mother at the Council's hand, specifically that of Victor Heatheros. By the end of the day, Mellia was welcomed as a 'caretaker' of the Satori.

10

As the sun drooped down, weighted by the soupy Scottish mist, Mellia trudged towards the Magic Market. Tired and hungry, Mellia felt lonelier than ever. She did not know how she would survive her father's combat class after her first day at the preserve.

She passed the Vivarium as the pixies were bespelling the heavy door closed. Mellia thought the pixies hadn't seen her plodding by, but as they flitted towards the market, Ashwing turned around and hissed at her, baring her teeth.

"Stay away from Janus, Monkey girl. They're mine," she said. The other pixies turned and scoffed at Mellia.

"What do they have to say about that?" Mellia mumbled. But the pixies had spread their wings and flown out of ear shot.

Mellia arrived last to the market, just as darkness swept over the remnants of the sunset. In the middle of a makeshift sandpit, her father stood ramrod straight, clad in his uniform. Medals sparkled in the glittering lanterns that surrounded the fighting pit. A weapon mount held all kinds of practice weapons, thick wooden steelwood staffs, wooden swords and blades, and maces and morning stars wrapped in cloth to protect the practicing troupe.

Mellia saw her roommates and the pixies staring raptly at her father, as well as the other keepers. He spoke just above a whisper, recounting a battle where he had defeated two Darkentine poachers by jumping over them and binding them with a rope spell before calling council wizards to jail the criminals.

"What about the time you lost my mother?" Mellia spat bitterly, refusing to join the circle of keepers that surrounded her father, eyes glazed with adoration.

The admiral flinched, showing a rare break in his stoicism. Ignoring the nervous gasps of the keepers, the admiral added smoothly, "All the more reason for you to learn to fight, my daughter."

Mellia scowled back, and she could feel Biko's uncertainty emanating from deep in her pocket. Biko felt loyalty to Mellia's father for rescuing him, but Mellia was his person.

Without further acknowledging his daughter, the admiral motioned for a large girl troll to choose a weapon and join him in the ring. She smoothed her rows of long braids and selected a heavy-looking morning star. She twirled, expertly playing to the crowd. The troll appeared to outweigh the admiral by at least one hundred pounds of pure muscle, and Mellia could see the beefy troll's thighs and biceps straining under her tunic.

"What's your name, Troll?" Jonathan asked. Raising his finger and using a spell, he drew a line of blue fire, indicating the perimeter of the fight. Frightened, a cluster of keepers jumped back, emptying the circle.

"Ripsider, sir," she responded sharply. "Four successful missions, sir. Elegons and Mandla Lions."

"Impressive, young lady. Ready for some live practice?"

"Will you be choosing a weapon, sir?" the troll asked.

The admiral responded with a small smile, shaking his head. "I won't need one."

Cocky, considering he lost my mother, Mellia thought, tasting the acid flavor of anger on her tongue.

As if that was an invitation to strike, the troll charged the admiral with surprising speed and efficiency, swinging the mace high above her head. The admiral stepped aside with practiced grace, allowing the troll to stumble past him, falling face first in the sand, singeing some of her braids in the blue spellfire.

Ripsider's dark brown face was crimson with anger, and white sand coated her sweating skin and salted her hair. Her mouth twisted in rage, quieting the hoots and friendly taunts of the other keepers. *Perfect,* Mellia thought, *my father is making just as many enemies here as I am.*

Ripsider whirled on the admiral, who feigned a bored yawn. He conjured a Blazeguard Whip between his thin fingers, magically pulling whip length from the air. He launched himself above the pit and flew circles around the befuddled and frustrated troll, using the whip like a lasso to bind her with her weapon trapped at her side.

The crowd clapped, and Ripsider growled, waddling out of the sand ring as the admiral wiggled his fingers, causing the spell rope to dissipate as though it had never existed.

"I appreciate your bravery, Ripsider. You will be a great warrior," the admiral called after the pouting troll.

"This week we will be learning the Blazeguard spell, which can be used to safely capture our enemies and bring them to Madstone for questioning," the admiral explained. "When you're trying to conjure a Blazeguard, think of weaving the spellfibers into rope used only to subdue."

Finally, something I can use to find my mother, Mellia thought, determined to learn the spell. The admiral lined the raggedy knot of amazed keepers and watched and coached as they tried to yank magic rope out of nothing. Mellia conjured some shimmering threads of spellfiber, but nothing cohesive.

Mellia noticed Sollix had wrapped himself up in a thin spellfiber twine and was straining to break free. The Admiral patted Janus on their back as they created a glittering and perfect Blazeguard, that resembled the admiral's whip. Mellia was stung when her father passed her without a word. Before she could attempt the elusive Blazeguard again, the Admiral clapped his hands.

"That's all for tonight. You are dismissed for dinner. Some of you did well," her father announced, offering a rare compliment. "Some of you need to do better. We will be practicing Blazeguards more, but sometimes that is not enough. These trainings will cover wand use and weapons. Great fighters use diverse methods," he added, looking at Mellia. She raised her chin, as her grandfather had taught her. *Always hold your chin high, don't ever look down*, he'd said.

"Mellia did me a solid favor yesterday when she rescued me. I was hanging off a Skvader headed for certain death in the Black Forest," Sollix said, pulling sticky loose strands of the remaining attempts of his failed Blazeguard spell off his robes. The admiral's eyes narrowed towards the distracted troll.

Sollix looked up with wide eyes, as though he had just realized he was back talking to a powerful wizard. "Sir..." he squeaked.

The admiral ignored his comment and waved the hungry keepers towards the banquet hall.

Janus grabbed Sollix's now sweating beefy hand and pulled him towards the dining hall. Mellia quickly followed, fearful of being left behind with her father after challenging him. At the same time, she wished he would call her back. He didn't.

11

After Mellia survived her first Satori shift without having her mind shredded and turning into a giant gnelf baby, a set of tools appeared, leaning against her bed. A note tied to a net on the end of a long pole read:

Good work on your first day. Here's a little something to help you keep the creek in the Satori glen free of leaves, just how they like it. And you certainly don't want to make them mad. Cheers, General Fret

Now fully equipped, the days seemed to blend into a tiring routine. One morning, after a chocolate croissant and a marshmallow latte, she located her leaf scooping net between the trolls' oversized rakes, propped against the side of the banquet hall. Sollix flipped his horn cleaning brush in the air and caught it behind his back. Mellia thought it resembled a giant toothbrush, but Sollix firmly insisted it was specialized for uniceros' horns.

They walked slowly, muscles aching from the prior night's training of learning to flip an attacker. Paired with Enna, who was a similar size, Mellia came away with deep scratches from the pixie's sharpened nails and teeth. Mellia felt for Sollix, who was limping after being tossed around by Ripsider. Janus paired with Jaya, and to the chagrin of the admiral, they gently lowered each other to the ground with perfect form.

As they passed Fret at the entrance to the animal enclosures, Mellia gave a small wave. Biko popped from her pocket, saluting the goblin. Fret waved them through, engrossed in the latest pixie romance novel. Janus loped to Fire Brand, while Sollix lumbered toward Molly's cage. Mellia chuckled watching Norman running against the Gauze fence, trying to throw his hefty body into air .

As she entered the Satori area, Mellia was grateful for the spring-feeling Bioweatherus spell. The cherry blossom grove was kept at a comfortable yet moist temperature that allowed the flowers to stay in bloom and the streams to remain flowing. Mellia stifled a laugh when she walked through the flowered archway of the enclosure.

The white and gray simians were lying on thick tree branches, their faces shoved in the pages of the latest elf fiction. When she crossed the threshold of the grove, the monkeys rushed to her, though they couldn't move quickly. They held her hands in their furry grip, checking her mind to see how her evening had gone.

One of the older female monkeys had bonded to Mellia. When Mellia crossed through the Satori threshold, the monkey would always greet her, pulling her hand towards her favorite soft, aged log. A seat-like groove had been worn into the fallen tree trunk.

The doting Satori's name was Nomi. She loved to pick imaginary lice from Mellia's hair and bring her giant, juicy beetles, which Mellia slipped to Biko. Nomi began trying to instruct Mellia on powers of telepathy. Because they couldn't always use words, it took a while for Mellia to learn her new friend's name. She was able to figure it out with Biko, after a long and frustrating game of practicing sounds with him.

Mellia felt her frustration building more and more daily. Mellia did not want to fail Nomi. She sat with the sweet and musty smelling monkey for hours, and her head felt like a swamp of honey, with no telepathic messages going in or out, except with Biko.

One day, as the sun was dropping down over the horizon, and the cherry blossom grove was growing dark, Mellia screamed in anger.

The monkeys startled, looking at their keeper in shock. They were used to each other's sloth-like movements and preferred consistent peace and quiet. Mellia motioned to Biko and stomped out of the grove. *You're not ready for it yet,* Biko explained to the frustrated gnelf. *They decide when and how to share their gift.*

That evening, the yeasty, comforting scent of fresh bread mingled with sweet aromas of warm, freshly baked cookies caused Mellia's stomach to growl as they entered the Great Banquet Hall. Sollix heard it and looked impressed. "Sammies tonight?" he joked, referring to the reincarnating dining hall pigs who cooked themselves each night.

"Still not that hungry," Mellia grumbled back. Mellia felt a twinge in her gut, and it wasn't the hunger. Sollix had stood up to her father for her on her first night of training, and he continued to be kind to her despite her prickly demeanor. *That's got to be worth something,* she thought guiltily, reevaluating her feelings about friendship. Reading her thoughts, she heard Biko snort in agreement from her pocket.

"Your loss." Sollix grinned and cut in front of her at the food line. "Grab me some of those macarons from the dessert table--you owe me for waking you up every morning. I was five minutes late to my shift. Luckily, I think Neathersby was occupied with other things, but I'm still on dessert restriction."

Mellia eyed the high tower of multicolored French cookies.

"Grab me a few of those vanilla ones," Sollix repeated with a mischievous wink. The troll looked hurt when Mellia ignored him. He grabbed a rack of ribs and slammed it down on his tray, avoiding looking at Mellia.

One of the floating ladles dished some gooey macaroni onto the troll's heaped platter. Sollix tipped his plate down, motioning for more, but the ladle waved him on, somehow looking both firm and strict. Sollix did not argue.

As Mellia sat down, Janus appeared next to her. They had their usual plate of rice and fish, which looked fresh and delicious. *I'll have to learn where they get that,* she thought, plunging her fork into her cheddar and brie macaroni and cheese.

Biko emerged from her pocket and grabbed some noodles. He stretched the cheese playfully in his tiny hands. Mellia could feel happiness radiating from the tiny monkey. He did love noodles.

After the meal, Janus abruptly spellaported back to their shared dormitory. Mellia and Sollix walked back to their room. The curtain of Scottish mist had parted, revealing the pale face of the moon and a diamond-studded sky. Sollix was unusually quiet. Mellia insides tugged guiltily.

Back at their room, Mellia said nothing to Janus and flopped down on the bed, facing the wall. After a few minutes, she saw some strange sparks flitting in front of her eyes. She turned her head and realized Janus was sending flickers of light towards her to get her attention.

"You are the most annoying wizard I've ever met," she grumbled. "What do you want?"

"Well, I have a gift for you. Should I just take it back, then?" they teased.

Mellia hopped up at the mention of a gift. Gnelves were notorious for loving any kind of present.

"Ho! I knew that would do it," Janus said, pulling an intricately carved knife from a sheath made of iridescent dragon scales. They plucked a silken strand of their hair and let it fall over the dagger. The hair split. Fully awake, Mellia jabbed her open hand towards them.

"Careful, gnelf," Janus warned. "That's a dwarf-forged diamond blade, the sharpest in the world, with a carved Gaiden bone handle. For a pip like you, your best bet is close combat."

Mellia marveled at the chiseled bone; gleaming carved dragons danced along the hilt. Her surprised expression reflected back at her in the flawless blade.

"Why would you give me this?" she asked.

"Look, gnelf. I see your pain every day. It comes out in your mean comments and the way you act. In Gaiden culture, when we see someone in pain, we give them a meaningful gift, no matter how awful they are. We believe sharing our gifts turns pain and anger into hope and joy."

Mellia's expression turned from surprise to chagrin. Her cheeks burned, and she felt her stomach whirling with sickening shame. She knew she hadn't been kind to her roommates. She heard Biko make a harrumph sound from where he perched on her dresser. She looked at Sollix, who returned her gaze with raised eyebrows and pursed lips. Mellia raised her chin and tried to think of a defensive response, but she couldn't.

Her chin began to wobble, and fresh tears burned her cheeks. At that moment, the glass ball of blackened grief burst inside of her. She cried for her mother, her father, and her grandfather. Janus took the knife from her hand and sheathed it, placing it on her dresser. They and Sollix embraced Mellia for some time, until finally, her heaving sobs became gentle.

When they released her, she said simply, "Thank you, and I'm sorry." Her roommates nodded at her silently, accepting her apology.

"Sollix, should we take her?" Janus asked, with a rare and huge grin. Sollix produced a porkchop from his robe pockets and ripped a hunk off the meat like a piece of bread. Janus looked at him with clear disdain.

"What? That was emotional. I'm eating my feelings right now. And what do you mean? Take her where?" the troll said through bites of meat.

Janus narrowed their eyes and placed their hands on their hips.

"Oh!" Sollix appeared to understand what Janus was hinting at. "Yes, I'm in. Wait, it's your turn to bring the treats," he said, taking another bite of chop to emphasize his point.

"Sorry, friend, these are new robes." Janus pretended to be apologetic as Sollix regretfully tucked the remaining bit of pork into a napkin and then into his robe.

About thirty minutes later, Mellia found herself on a roof ledge of the castle wall that faced outward towards Loch Ness. She could see the moon reflecting off the lake, which flickered as Nessie, the sea dragon, splashed the water with her tail. With her gnome sense, she could smell the woody, fibrous trees of the Black Forest as well as the clean, fresh brine of the lake water. The sounds of crickets and other night chirpers were a quiet orchestra.

"Best view in the whole place," Janus bragged, leaning against a maniacally grinning stone gargoyle. Mellia recognized the Guardgoyle from the front gate.

"Right, Winston?" Janus elbowed the marble statue.

"That's for sure, chap," a high-pitched voice responded in a thick British accent. Mellia jumped, and she could hear Biko chuckling from her pocket. Sollix pointed to a tiny plaque attached to the castle wall.

Captain Sir Winston F. Appleton-Langdon
First Flight Battalion in the War of Roses
Head Guardgoyle for the Preserve of Enchanted Creatures
His gray marbled head swiveled towards the Loch.

Janus grinned and explained, "Winston is in love with Nessie, but only from afar. As the head Guardgoyle, he cannot leave the castle grounds without turning back to unmovable stone."

"She's a bonnie lass, my Nessie," Winston said lovingly. Sollix produced the pork from his pockets and tossed it in the air. Dirt and moss sprayed from Winston's pedestal as he jumped up, catching the slab in his wide, toothy mouth.

"Very good. I won't tell Neathersby you are all up here so close to curfew time," Winston promised, chewing loudly.

Bribe complete, Sollix and Janus sat down on the castle ledge and motioned for Mellia to join them.

"How did you find this place?" Mellia asked, staring up at the black sky blanket bejeweled with diamond bright stars. The bustle of the preserve center receded as the keepers retired to their rooms after dinner.

"Mellia, I've been here for a long time," Janus said. "You're not the only one who has a story." Mellia could hear the usual sarcasm and humor in Janus's voice turn tight and pained.

"He's Gaiden," Sollix added, as if that cleared anything up. Mellia knew Gaiden were sacred and spiritual dragon protectors. She had never met one, and she suddenly had a new appreciation for the Chinese wizard. Sollix cleared his throat, as if to explain Gaiden further, and looked at Janus. Janus shook their head sadly, indicating they would tell their own story.

"The Gaiden believe that male sorcerers should work with the male dragons, while the women sorceresses are assigned to the female dragons. When a child turns ten years old, they are separated into male and female houses. When I turned ten, I refused to go to either house. Angry that I was breaking tradition, my father and mother agreed to cast me out."

Janus finished their story, falling into silence. Mellia and Biko felt Janus's sadness without any use of telepathy. Mellia was surprised when Biko jumped from her shoulder and curled up under Janus's chin. The young Satori used his tail to wipe the silent tears cascading down the Gaiden's lovely face.

12

Later that night, Mellia wrote a letter to her grandfather back at home in Palenque.

Dear Abuelo,

I miss you so much! I miss Mama. I miss your pozole legendario. Have you heard anything about her? I haven't. I worry all the time.

I do have some good news, Abuelo. I met some friends, Janus and Sollix.

Head Gamekeeper Neathersby assigned me to the Satori. The first day was really hard, Abuelo. They took me to a memory where I saw when Mama was kidnapped. I have been trying to learn telepathy and how to control my enemy's mind. I can't get it. It's been days. What do I do, Abuelo?

Sollix and Janus think we will be assigned to a mission soon.

Ok, it's getting late. Te amo.

Mellia

P.S. Can we please have some of your famous hot chocolate the second I get home?

Janus helped her spellaport it to her grandfather. In the morning, Mellia found a letter had appeared on her dresser. She recognized her grandfather's neat, fluid handwriting. He had used her mother's nickname for her. Alejandra had called her "Little Mink," because she was smart, small, and tough.

Dear Little Mink,

I miss you, too. The hacienda is so quiet without you. I haven't heard from your mom, and I worry for her every day.

Funny you should ask about the Satori. I worked with Kaga Hibiki, a very respected Satori. During the Battle of Neer, I was able to connect with him once for a brief second. He told me to think of every possible thing at once, and then my mind would clear. Though Satori are able to communicate freely without making contact with touch, you will not have that power.

Try it, but be careful, Querida, because mind reading and controlling others is a dangerous power.

As we both know from painful experience, missions are dangerous, so I hope you know who you can trust. I have been in contact with your father. He misses you, and he is lost. I hope you can mend your quarrel with him.

I'm off to gather some Aile today. Wish me luck!

Te amo.

Abuelo

P.S. I will have as much chocolate as you and little Biko can drink.

When Mellia put the letter down, Janus quietly prodded her with the back of their hairbrush. Mellia looked around confused in the darkness, wiping the sleep from her heavy eyes.

"It's still dark. What are you doing, Wizard?" she grumbled.

"I'm going to teach you how to fight. Then what can your father say? Come on, get up," Janus ordered.

Mellia stumbled into her robes as Biko and Sollix snored in unison. She followed Janus down to the chilly shores of Loch Ness. Janus had set up a weapons rack and hung lanterns that cut through the cold mist. They drew a circle in the sand with their pointer finger, just as her father had the first night at the Preserve. Despite the darkness, Mellia could see Nessie's golden eyes glowing close to the shore of the lake.

Janus placed their hands out in front of them. They seemed to be kneading the air, almost as though they were stretching an invisible strand of toffee. Mellia watched in amazement as a red Blazeguard whip appeared in front of her. Looking serious, Janus whipped it at her. She heard Nessie chuff with anticipation for the pending fight. The sharp tip of Janus's Blazeguard sliced through her thick purple robes as she dodged out of the way.

"What the..." Before Mellia could finish her sentence, Janus cracked his Blazeguard, this time nearly slashing her leg.

"We are out here to fight, no? Do you think you'll have a chat before a battle with one of the Darkentine poachers?" Janus said, snapping the red whip again, reinforcing their point. Mellia was light and quick on her gnelf feet. She leapt over Janus, avoiding the Blazeguard's painful sting.

"When are you going to show me how to conjure one?" Mellia said as she landed behind Janus, just out of the magic whip's reach. "That would make this a fair fight."

"Good point. I can't leave you defenseless," Janus replied. They turned to face Mellia. She copied their motion and stretched her hands out in front of her. Nothing happened at first. Mellia wiggled her fingers and waved her hands around, feeling frustrated.

"I'll never get this. How do you do it so easily?" Mellia shouted at Janus, tears pricking at the sides of her eyes. They placed their hands over hers, calming her frantic motion. "I think about what justice would be for me," they said softly.

Mellia closed her eyes and thought about catching Victor Heatheros. She moved her hands in the same invisible toffee stretching gesture, and she felt something tangible between her fingers. Her Blazeguard was black and thick, writhing with dark shadows. She flung the long strands towards Janus. He flipped backwards, attempting to dodge her attack, but her whip wrapped itself around Janus's wrist.

"Ha! Victory, Wizard!" she shouted gleefully. She heard Nessie whimper.

"Mellia, get it off, it burns," Janus said in a low voice, their eyes closed in pain. She dropped her magic weapon, and it disappeared, a sinking, inky dark shadow in the white sand. Janus looked at her as if they had never seen her before. "That's not what a Blazeguard is supposed to do," they said. "Let's call it a day."

As they headed back to their rooms, Mellia could feel Janus's concerned gaze drilling into her back.

In the banquet hall, Sollix began to take his morning tea with Jaya, the Owltender and his love interest. Mellia and Janus joined them. Mellia smiled at Jaya, and he smiled back. Mellia loved Jaya's soft lilting voice and his stories about growing up in India.

"Coming by the Owlery today?" Jaya asked Mellia.

"Yep, fresh out of books. Good thing the historical fiction section is so vast-- those monkeys are fast readers!" She motioned towards her brown leather satchel, bulging with novels to return.

13

Full of pastries, with a caramel steamed cappuccino for Mellia and tea for the rest, the group split up. Mellia smirked watching Sollix stare at Jaya as he walked away with Janus. The stroll to the Owlery was short, and Mellia bragged about Sollix the whole time.

"You know, Jaya, Sollix is super strong. But he also has this beautiful singing voice."

Jaya nodded serenely without commenting. Mellia could never get the Owltender to admit his feelings, no matter how hard she boasted.

Even though she spent a few hours a week gathering books for the Satori in the Owlery, Mellia was amazed with the spectacle. The humongous redwood tree was hollow at the bottom, with a book check out area manned by gnelves, wizards, dwarfs and other beings fortunate enough to have been chosen by owls to be Owltenders.

After Jaya helped her check out her books, Mellia headed straight to the Satori, and like most of the keepers, Mellia jogged around the perimeter of their enclosure to make sure she could see no weaknesses in the magic that shielded the creatures. *Probably the most important thing you can do,* Janus had explained to her earlier that week.

Biko rode on Mellia's shoulder as she crossed the threshold of the Satori enclosure. It seemed darker than usual, and the Satori were not waiting at the front to ransack her bookbag. *It's time,* Biko warned her. *Don't be scared.* She then felt the strong, soft hands of the Satori urging her into the depth of the grove, pushing her from behind so she could not see them. Biko was pulled from her shoulder, and he whimpered as they were separated.

The Satori pushed her into a dark, dank corner of the grove. She saw a cherry tree with blackened blossoms and riveted black trunk. A deep hollow gaped like a toothless mouth at the base of the tree. Mellia managed to whirl out of the insistent grip of the Satori. She saw four of the bigger, elder simians, including Nomi, faces painted with thick charcoal paste.

Pushing her into the hollow, the four elder Satori entered. Mellia struggled to breathe in the dark space, and her heart pounded rapidly. *Sit down,* Nomi communicated. Surrounded by the pungent animals, Mellia sat and closed her eyes. Nomi gave the next direction: *Push us out.* Mellia wasn't sure what the elderly monkey meant until she felt the familiar itch inside of her head.

Images of Enna the pixie baring her fangs and hissing, her father's disapproving gaze, and her mother's disappearance pounded her like a torrential rain. She sobbed and held her head, trying to make the Satori stop. *Push us out,* Nomi yelled. Mellia felt her good memories slipping away, replaced by an echoing disapproval in her father's tone, and her mother's cry for help. One thousand Ennas hissed at her. Her head began to ache, as though her brain was swelling out of her skull.

Just as she thought she would go completely insane, she saw an image of her grandfather. *Think of everything at once,* he reminded her gently. Mellia forced herself to follow her grandfather's advice. A calm, cool darkness soothed her aching head. She felt the Satori's presence recede, and she drove them from her mind.

Nice job, Child, Nomi said, rubbing her back and wiping her tears with the back of her fuzzy hand. *Now reach into my head and find my worst fears and memories.*

"Nomi, I could never do that to you! Please don't ask me to." Mellia gripped the monkey's rough hand. *Do it, Mellia.* Mellia forced her mind to think about everything all at once, and she squeezed Nomi's hand. She saw a shiny red cord in her mind's eye, connecting her to Nomi. Focusing on the red strand, she could see into Nomi's mind. The images whirled back to her, almost overwhelming her.

Choose one, Nomi thought at Mellia, sounding strained. Mellia picked one, the impressions of a tiny Nomi falling into a deep pool in the cherry blossom glen, and not being able to swim out. Her little arms flailed, and she kicked her legs, just barely above the water line. Nomi's hand trembled in Mellia's. *Replay it,* Nomi said. Mellia hesitated but brought the memory back and repeated it.

In the dark hollow, Mellia could feel Nomi's body shaking. The other Satori shifted uncomfortably. Nomi began gasping for air, and Mellia felt another Satori's grip on her hand, pulling it off of Nomi and breaking the connection.

"Nomi! Nomi! I'm so very sorry. Are you okay? Please tell me you're okay," Mellia whimpered, horrified.

Still out of breath, Nomi replied, *I am fine. That was a very good job. You made it so real.*

That evening in the dining hall, Mellia and Enna reached for the same roll of bread in a basket. Their hands touched just long enough for Mellia to see some of her thoughts. Mellia felt frightened; inside the pixie's mind circled vicious and dark thoughts. Mellia could see that the pixie was in love with Janus, and she was envious that Mellia had befriended them. Her thoughts were chaotic and colored with a green and black haze.

Enna jerked away from Mellia, taking the roll and shoving her back. Biko hopped from Mellia's pocket and hissed at the pixie, sensing Mellia's surprise. Enna bared sharp teeth and snarled back, her pupils becoming snakelike slits. Biko refused to back down, fisting his paws as though preparing to box.

Tedar, a giant troll, lumbered up to the table, reaching his long and muscled arm between Mellia and Enna. "Excuse me, ladies," Tedar said, shooting a cocky and flirtatious grin towards Enna. "Just grabbing a roll."

As though she had been acting in a play, Enna's face relaxed into the usual flirty and vapid expression Mellia had become accustomed to. Enna smiled flirtatiously at the troll, twirled her silver blond hair, and stroked his beefy bicep. The two strutted together back to the tight knot of their friends at the other end of the table.

14

———

Sollix's high pitched and wet sneeze interrupted Mellia's thoughts as the morning sun rose over the Loch and pierced the arched castle window. The troll was shivering feverishly, shaking his sturdy bedposts. He had caught a troll cold going around the preserve dormitories, and he had been bedridden for the last two days. Mellia winked at Sollix, bringing him the tea tray left outside their door, by a certain handsome Owltender.

"I'll stop and check in on Molly and Norman," Mellia promised Sollix. "Freshen up their wheat grass."

Sollix nodded, massaging the top of his nose. In a voice that sounded both croaky and brittle at once, he said, "No, I couldn't bother you to do that." Mellia rolled her eyes.

"Just tell me what to do," the gnelf insisted, putting her hands on her hips stubbornly.

"Do not approach them from the front." Sollix wheezed and sipped some tea, with as much drama as he could muster.

About an hour later, under the tepid heat of the Plains, Mellia found herself centered in front of Molly. The three-ton uniceros grunted just as Mellia remembered her troll friend's warning. The large black eyes on the side of the beast's head narrowed.

Before Mellia could dodge, Molly closed her enormous, slobbery, hippo-like mouth around Mellia's waist. Molly's hot breath smelled bitterly of chewed leaves and unbrushed teeth. With a surprisingly graceful flick of her jaw, Molly released Mellia, tossing her ten feet into the air.

Mellia landed hard on her back with a huge thud that jarred her bones. Slipping in the slimy mud of the enclosure, Mellia dodged the massive hooves pounding inches from her head by rolling to the side of the pen.

Molly, the uniceros, fixed her angry gaze on the tiny gnelf, lowering her head. Mellia was nearly blinded by Molly's horn, a shimmering golden rod jutting from the center of the uniceros's bulky skull. Mellia knew from Sollix that the horn was pointed enough to slide right through her innards like butter under a warm knife.

As the uniceros began to gallop forward at surprising speed for her girth, Mellia recovered from the impact and jumped over the 10-foot fence. She felt the ground shudder as the angry uniceros slammed her bulky, scaled frame into the impenetrable Gauze barrier.

Just as quickly as she was angered, the uniceros lost interest and ambled away towards her wagon-sized food trough of peeled green peas and wheat grass.

Wrinkling her nose, Mellia poked her long, thin finger through a new hole in her already tattered and faded purple robes. She was covered in thick black mud from the slimiest part of the uniceros's pen. It caked on her robes and tall boots. Just as Mellia took a deep breath in relief, a dark shadow eclipsed her. Her hand flicked to the dagger strapped to her left bicep.

"No need for a knife, Child," a very Scottish voice said.

Mellia looked up to see Head Gamekeeper Neathersby blocking out the sky. Neathersby smelled of tobacco, sweat, and, oddly, rose petals. Her mouth was pulled into a taut line. "Basic uniceros, Kelgwyn," Neathersby chided.

"Approach them from the side. I know." Mellia looked down, willing herself not to cry.

"Chin up, Kelgwyn. I appreciate you filling in for Sollix. You're starting to fit in here." Neathersby gave the compliment with what may have been a smile, but it looked more like a painful grimace.

Not one to dawdle, Neathersby turned sharply on her heel and marched towards the Fire Brand. Mellia was stunned; the Gamekeeper had not spoken that many words to her in the entirety of her time at the preserve.

Mellia felt a rare emotion: pride. She did feel like she was fitting in. *I should have asked her about my mother*, Mellia thought, watching the cyclops march stiffly away.

Mellia spent a little more time brushing Molly's horn and playing with Norman. She ran back to her room a bit early to change her tattered robes, slimy with uniceros paste and Norman's slobber. After she bathed, she found fresh robes in her drawer and wondered what kind of magical system did the laundry for her. She strapped the dagger to her arm, concealing it under the voluminous robe sleeve. Biko waved as she rushed out the door.

She felt ready for combat. *My father is not proud of me, but Neathersby and my friends are. That's something*, she thought, lifting her chin as he passed by the lineup of young keepers, preparing for practice in the sand circle. Her father's eyes squinting with icy appraisal.

"Tonight, we will be working on hand-to-hand combat. Punches, blocks, elbows," the admiral announced. "Ripsider, come on up."

Jonathan proceeded to parry and block Ripsider's dangerous and heavy punches. He threw some feints of his own, confusing the troll. He ended the demonstration and paired up partners. Sollix groaned when he was partnered with Ripsider again.

"She's too good!" he moaned.

Enna strutted across from Mellia, holding her sharp nails in front of her face, taunting the gnelf. Mellia hissed at her, imitating the pixie's threat.

"Spar!" Jonathan shouted. The participants stood in two parallel lines facing each other. The sand pit became a flurry of activity as the keepers swung punches and parried.

"Bend your knees!" the admiral coached. "Counter with your left."

Enna attacked. Instead of a closed fist near Mellia's face, she formed her hand into a claw and scratched. Surprised, Mellia forgot to block. She put her hand over the bleeding gouges as spikes of anger prodded her insides.

"Enna, too much," Janus chided, pausing their own sparring match. The pixie smiled demurely at them.

"Sorry, didn't mean to scratch your girlfriend," she taunted, breathing heavily with excitement. The admiral said nothing but watched intently.

She parried another of Enna's wild onslaughts. This time Enna was able to rake the other side of Mellia's face with her left hand. Mellia's vision darkened, and she felt herself succumbing to rage.

Enna attacked again, and Mellia grabbed her wrist and bent it back. With her contact, she closed her eyes and found the red cord that connected her to Enna's mind. Mellia found a moment to use her new skills against the vicious pixie.

A very young Enna stood in the forest with her head down. A large, red-faced lady pixie stood over her. Mellia couldn't hear what she was saying, but she saw spittle flying from her lips. The larger pixie looked just like an older version of Enna, and Mellia assumed it was her mother. The woman pointed down, screaming, at the terrified child pixie.

Mellia felt Enna's sadness and fear. She prepared her mind to repeat the image to Enna on a loop.

Something stopped her. *This isn't me*, Mellia thought, pulling back the red thread.

"Enough," the admiral shouted. The pixie sunk to her knees, Mellia still twisting her wrist. Shocked at her father's reprimand, she dropped Enna's arm. "Control yourself, Mellia."

Mellia's body sagged under the weight of her father's furious gaze. Enna looked like a broken doll, still kneeling.

"Ashwing, Dewlane, Mandala, take Enna to the Aid Tent to get checked by Caduceus," he ordered, fully back in control. "Mellia, for the rest of class, you can watch the others from the bench over there. Maybe by watching others fight with honor, you will learn to as well."

Cheeks burning red with anger, guilt, and embarrassment, Mellia stomped over to the nearby bench and sat down with an audible huff.

15

That night, Mellia's body was covered in bruises like Sollix's sometimes was. The stains on her robes matched his. Sollix had recovered from his flu, but was now aching with the aftermath of Ripsider's excessively strong punches. Janus brought them both soup as they lay in their beds moaning about the states of their sore bodies. Janus rolled their eyes and sat at their mirror brushing their hair.

"Ooh! I almost forgot," Mellia said.

She reached into one of her coat pockets and tossed a thumb-sized bag of herbs to Sollix. It was a magicked mixture of arnica and dragon plants from deep in the Palenque. Her grandfather had sent her with a huge pouch when she spellaported to the preserve. As she mixed the herbs into her soup, she remembered her grandfather's downtrodden face at the gates of the Hacienda as he held her hand, preparing her to spellaport.

"Pungent!" Sollix commented, interrupting Mellia's reverie. His lips puckered as he slurped some leafy broth.

"Drink it all, Troll, so it works," Mellia warned.

A heavy rap from the door knocker startled them all; Janus even dropped their brush. Janus spellaported to the door, looking cautiously through the peephole.

Their eyes widened. "It's General Fret," they whispered.

As Janus opened the door, General Fret marched into the room. He was still somehow intimidating, even clad in striped pink and white silk pajamas with a matching tasseled sleeping cap.

"Gamekeeper Neathersby has summoned the three of you. Report to her office immediately." With his message delivered, Fret did not wait for the trio to respond and spellaported away.

"A mission!" Sollix and Janus exclaimed at the same time. Janus pulled on their red hanfu, Sollix donned a thick wool pea coat and a cap, and Mellia wrapped herself in her fur parka. Excitedly, Sollix and Janus exchanged ideas as they walked across the campus.

"Maybe they will send us to catch another uniceros or to protect a herd of Elegons," the two mused.

Mellia pet Biko nervously in her coat. She could feel Biko trying to soothe her.

Neathersby's office was at the top of one of the castle turrets. The swirling staircase was dark, cold, and drafty. Mildew clung to the stone walls, banisters, and steps, making everything feel slimy.

"This is why I spellaport," Janus said, wrinkling their nose and holding their robes tight to their body. The robe dragons were curled in tight golden balls, trying to avoid the dankness.

Two flights of stairs before the top of the turret, Mellia stopped. She put a finger to her lips. Her elfen hearing picked up Neathersby and Fret arguing.

"They are too young and inexperienced, Nalina. You are sending them to their deaths," Fret growled.

Mellia's eyes grew wide as she strained her ears.

"You're missing the point, General. The Council will never see this coming. I haven't told anyone that I have this plan, besides the admiral and the Guild. We promised that the preserve would take care of the crane issue. You know Ironin trusts us to handle business," Neathersby answered.

"The Darkentine ruffians have spies everywhere, Nalina. Even here," Fret said, and Mellia could hear the worry softening his gruff tones.

"They can handle it, Fret. They have powers they haven't even discovered yet. Have faith...It's not nice to eavesdrop!" Neathersby's voice rose at the end.

Looking ashamed, Mellia, Sollix, and Janus rushed up the stairs, stumbling into Neathersby's office. The room at the top of the turret was deceptively small, and to Mellia's surprise, the walls were covered in photographs of Neathersby with various famous wizards. Mellia had not pegged the Gamekeeper as sentimental.

"There's my dad!" Sollix said, pointing to a picture behind Neathersby's desk. A regal troll in a leopard skin robe stared back at whomever was wielding the camera. Zulkis Xukundi, King of the Zimbabwean Trolls, stood next to a younger-looking Neathersby.

Mellia noticed another picture of the ginger-haired cyclops standing with Mellia's mother and father. Her father had his usual serious pursed lips and hawk eyes, while her mother looked soft with warm eyes. They were all dressed in military gear.

There was yet another picture of Mellia's mom with Mellia's grandfather, both of their chins tilted up proudly. She didn't say anything, but she thought of her grandfather's words about her father. She refused to let herself cry. Instead, she admired Sollix's parents' regal appearance. Neathersby waited patiently.

When the trio had finished admiring the photographs, Neathersby motioned for them to sit in the three chairs in front of her desk.

"Are we going on a mission?" Sollix asked, his voice rising an octave with excitement.

Looking at her eager friend, Mellia could picture how Sollix must have looked as a child. Round, coffee-colored eyes widened with excitement, and his cheeks plumped with his big smile. Neathersby steepled her long calloused fingers, resting her elbows on her desk. She nodded. Sollix and Janus exchanged wide-eyed gazes.

"This is going to be dangerous. Are you sure you're up for it?" Neathersby looked intensely at Mellia. She shifted in her seat, thinking of her mother. Mellia nodded, trying to appear confident, but with her emotions roiling, she was too afraid to speak.

Neathersby flicked her fingers, creating a holospell; golden lights swirled over her desk, sparking and twirling. A scene of light began to take shape. Mellia could see an old man sitting on the edge of a pond. She saw cherry trees forming a glen around him. Elegant birds glided over the pond and rested regally on the shore. They did not look like regular birds, but angular, crane-like creatures.

"Are those birds origami?" Mellia asked, almost entranced by the scene before her.

"The elusive origami cranes of Mount Yoshino," Neathersby answered. "They hold the spell to immortality. The venerable Wizard Takeji drew the ancient words to the spell on the cranes himself, even before I was born. We have received word from our spies that Dark-entine Poachers are planning to take the cranes to decode their immortality spells. You can only imagine the chaos that would occur if that actually happened. Your mission is to save the cranes and bring them back here under our protection."

The golden light version of Takeji waved up at the astonished group. Neathersby tipped her hat. Janus' eyes grew even wider. A small trio of wizards shaped with black shadows had entered the peaceful glen. In unison, they aimed their wands at the sitting figure of light, Takeji. Darkness poured from their wands, disintegrating the entire luminous scene, and it went out as quickly as it had appeared.

Mellia thought she could see a look of pain on Takeji's glowing face before he was gone. The trio was speechless, and Mellia noticed that Sollix was tongue tied for the first time since she had met him.

After a moment, Janus asked, "Why would you send the three of us after something as valuable as an immortality spell? Mellia is brand new." They raised a sculpted eyebrow suspiciously. "And what about Takeji?"

"Takeji can handle himself," Neathersby assured the Gaiden.

"Wait, isn't that the place where my mother was kidnapped?" Mellia asked, feeling her heart pounding. The forced memories from her first day with the Satori were burned into her mind. Mellia recognized the trees and the pond even in Neathersby's holospell. "If we accept this mission, will we find clues to where the Darkentine Council is holding her?"

"You just may find what you're looking for," Neathersby answered mysteriously, avoiding her desperate query.

"You leave in two weeks...by boat. There are too many Darkentine poachers out there to risk spellaporting you to the island. Unfortunately, they have learned to track spellaportation across long distances. General Fret, please weaponize our young friends."

Sollix's and Janus's childish exuberance returned, and they leapt out of their chairs, running Fret down and almost forgetting to say goodbye to Neathersby. Fret snapped his fingers, and the group found themselves in what Mellia came to understand was The Armory.

16

There was a gilded sign at the far end of the mission room that read: "A brave soul may feel fear, but they are braver upon conquering it." The letters seemed to glow with fire in the torchlight of the windowless room.

Mellia's eyes adjusted to the dim lighting--even half elves had excellent vision both during the brightest day and in the darkest moonlit night. Glass cases lined the walls of the dank cellar, and there was a simple rectangular steelwood table in the middle of the room with three plain brown satchels laying empty.

"Though you have learned the Blazeguard spell to disable poachers, you will need weapons for your journey. Some creatures are too big to Blazeguard, and others are too fast," General Fret explained.

Sollix smiled and replied, "Not for me."

Fret rolled his eyes and checked his gold watch.

"I need my beauty sleep. Let's do this. Which weapons speak to you?" General Fret asked. "These armaments seek out their guardian, not the other way around. The admiral will attempt to train you over the next few days," the General added, and Mellia heard doubt in his voice.

Sollix opened the glass cover of a case filled with shiny heavy metal and wood weaponry. The first thing he picked up was a morning star that sparked when he twirled it around. He pretended he was battling with someone and waved it towards Fret. A metal spike whizzed by Fret's ear.

"Wicked! Shoots spikes!" he shouted with glee.

"Careful, Troll! That's not a child's toy," Fret snarled as he ripped the weapon from Sollix's hands. He put a bony green finger to his lips, and whispered, "Shh."

The pointed ball at the end of the morning star shrunk to a tiny metal ball, and its spikes snapped inside of it. The handle and chain decreased to a palm-sized version of the maiming weapon.

"Aww, it's cute. Travel-sized," Janus joked. Sollix closed his fist around it and slipped it into his bag.

"Your turn, Wizard," Sollix grunted, annoyed with his friend's ribbing.

Janus glided around the room. Their pointed ears were twitching, trying to listen to which weapon called to them. There was a corner of the room filled with different thin and elegant wands, bulbous bejeweled scepters, and gnarled wooden staffs. Janus gravitated there.

A scepter with a red stone at the end jumped into their hand. Janus let a rare and goofy grin slip out. They held the scepter in front of them, and a graceful arc of contained fire burst forth, heating the room.

"This is the one!" they exclaimed.

Fret nodded. "Very good. That's a powerful scepter called Scorchvine, forged by a Gaiden like yourself hundreds of years ago. I'm not surprised."

"What does it do? I mean, besides making me hotter than I already am," Janus asked with a cheeky grin, flipping their hair. They held the scepter up to their robe, checking to see if it matched.

"It creates fire, and the stronger the wizard, the more damage it can do. To a true Gaiden, like yourself, the scepter can summon a dragon."

"Too bad I'm not a true Gaiden," Janus grumbled back.

"A true Gaiden is a state of being, not a location, Child," Fret chided, in a kinder voice than his normal gruff growl. Janus just rolled their eyes.

They all turned to Melia, who felt lost. She stood in front of the cabinet most likely meant for elves, filled with elegant bow and arrow sets, long thin swords, and even enchanted flutes. Nothing attempted to stab her or even wiggle in her direction.

She sighed and moved to a case filled with gnomish magic--potions, rune stones, and tied bundles of dried herbs. Nothing rustled her way.

Fret shifted the weight on his silken slippered feet. "Come on, Girl, I don't have all night."

As tears threatened to fall, she felt the warm and gentle presence of Sollix and Janus behind her. Janus whispered, "Mellia, just be you. You're not just an elf or just a gnome. Let go of that."

Mellia squeezed her eyes shut. She forced back her tears and took a deep breath. With her eyes still closed, she let her mind go silent of the constant doubt and worry.

Janus was right, of course. Keeping her harsh thoughts at bay, Mellia listened to the silence in the room and thought about the powers she did have--leaping and healing and spell casting and animal affinity...

From the far side of the room, she heard a rustle. She opened her eyes, and one of the glass cases had opened for her. A light shone out, illuminating the room. Sollix wrinkled his nose at a spider sliding down its thin gossamer line of web, illuminated by the glow of Mellia's object.

She rushed over and found a simple golden ring with an embedded white stone, swirled with ribbons of deep onyx. The stone was a perfect globe, jutting over its golden setting. It fit on the slender fourth finger of Mellia's hand.

Fret stepped back, looking at Mellia with reverence rather than his usual authoritative glare. "The Lifebender Ring," he murmured in awe. "That takes a powerful being indeed to manage. When used properly, it can bring the newly deceased back to life. It can also permanently destroy life, in a way that no magic can fix."

Mellia looked at the simple ring. It was pretty to look at, but it wasn't shooting spikes or creating arcs of fire. She tried waving her hand around and pointing her finger. Nothing. Mellia felt her helplessness return.

Now that each of the travelers had their magical item, Fret opened drawers and mumbled about missing potions. He shoved a map and a shield in Sollix's satchel, some vials of uniceros paste, herbs, and runes in Mellia's bag, and a pot and cooking seasonings in Janus's satchel, giving them a wink. Fret tossed Mellia a plain, large glass bottle with a stopper.

"That's a StreamDeep bottle. If you fill it with sea water and shake it vigorously, it will turn to fresh stream water from the Falls of Clyde. Used it myself when I used to go on missions," Fret explained, looking fondly at the bottle.

"Wait," Sollix cried before Fret could wiggle his fingers and spellaport them to their room. "What's my morning star's name? Mellia and Janus got names for their things."

"Norma." Fret smirked, and in a blink, the trio found themselves standing in the middle of their dorm room, as though they had never left in the first place.

Instead of heading to sleep, Sollix began playing with Norma, growing her and shrinking her until Janus gave him a look. Mellia laid in bed, snuggling with Biko, and though she was dreading more intense training with her father, she surprised herself by being able to fall asleep right away.

17

If there's something I still admire about my father, it's how impeccable he is even this early in the morning, Mellia thought grudgingly to herself. Jonathan stood in the center of the sand combat circle in his high-collared blue military uniform, gleaming with polished brass buttons and golden medals. His hair lay flat against his back in the style of elfen military, and his face appeared grim and emotionless.

"Look sharp, you three," Jonathan barked as the trio stumbled up. Janus and Sollix straightened their backs. Mellia stared defiantly back at her father. She had taken to wearing the dagger Janus had gifted her, tucked in the sheath strapped to her arm. She rubbed the hilt for comfort.

"This training is a matter of life and death. You will be facing Victor Heatheros, the most notorious member of the Darkentine Council. I cannot figure out why Neathersby thinks sending you after immortality spells is a good idea, but she outranks me, and she has the backing of the Guild," the admiral lectured, avoiding Mellia's gaze.

"So, we have a ridiculously short time to prepare you. Troll, we will start with you. What's your name and what is your weapon?" he ordered.

"Sollix, Sir. Son of Xulkis Stephen and Zulraja Kina Zukundi. The morning star named Norma chose me," Sollix said in a deep, soldiery voice.

"Ahh, so you are the youngest Zakundi. I fought with your father in the Ice Wars in Russia, many years ago. He is a great warrior, but not one for the cold," the admiral said, attempting a smile that looked more like a thin-lipped grimace to Mellia.

"Gaiden, I know you already. You have demonstrated excellent combat skills and effective wizardry during our sessions. I see you have Scorchvine; very nice." Janus held the ruby scepter out in front of them with their palms open. The red stone glowed in his hands.

Mellia's father gazed down at her, and she raised her fist, allowing her ring to catch the morning light. "The Lifebender Ring," was all he said, looking grimmer. Mellia clenched her jaw and pushed down a knot of anger rising in her chest.

"Well, let's dance," the admiral said, flexing his hands and summoning blue sparks between his fingers. Despite their amateur skills, the admiral did not go easy on the trio.

"Control Norma's spikes! Manifest where you want the points to land," the admiral shouted at Sollix as he hovered in the air above a cluster of flying morning star needles. Sollix was madly swinging the weapon above his head and yelling Sanzembe battle cries. The admiral erected a human-shaped target dummy made from hay and wood on one end of the sand circle.

"Just hit this, Troll," Jonathan commanded, rubbing the bridge of his nose in frustration. "And please, without the dramatic yelling."

Eagerly, Sollix whirled around, continuing to miss his target. But he was at least flinging spikes away from the rest of the group. It was Janus's turn next, and it was as though they'd had Scorchvine for decades.

With a bit of spell coaching from the admiral, Janus created perfect arches, bolts, and bullets of red fire. The light from the blaze and the burning ruby lit up the circle in the low morning dawn. Mellia saw a look of pride on her father's face. For a moment she longed for his praise before her seething anger returned.

"I hit it!" Sollix cried out. A cluster of Norma's spikes were driven into the edges of the target. Most of the barbs had hit the steelwood panel of the nearby Toad in the Hole Meat Pie Shop. Janus clapped for their friend. Mellia rolled her eyes and waited with a sigh.

Her father approached her and placed his long thin hands on her shoulders. She did not want to admit that she missed her father's strength.

"The Lifebender Ring is not so much a weapon as it is a choice. When the time comes, you will be offered an option to take a life or save a life," the admiral explained.

"That's it?" Mellia snarled. "I want to fight with my friends." *Someone has to save my mother,* she thought.

"Mellia, you have many other powers. Let's see your Blazeguard," the admiral said, remaining calm. Mellia placed her hands out and began making the weaving motion through the air.

Black coils of spellfiber manifested before her. She could smell the greasy cirrus, and it smelled like a capybara corpse she had come across in the jungle. She felt Janus's worried gaze on her back as they paused their fire making to watch.

"Stop!" Jonathan yelled sharply. "Mellia, your spellfiber is dark magic, made from anger and hatred. You must never manifest magic with anger."

"How else am I supposed to feel? Mom is missing, and you either ignore me or remind me of everything I'm doing wrong." She hurled her words at him, and the dark spellfiber ball grew bigger, seeming to thrive on the argument.

Jonathan clapped his hands together, producing an orb of white light that swallowed the dark magic spell Mellia had conjured.

"Magic training is over for today," the admiral said in a clipped tone. "You can head to the Great Banquet Hall to eat, and I will see you back here for hand-to-hand combat."

The two weeks passed in a blur of kickboxing, knife throwing, combat spell casting, wrestling, and learning defense. The admiral remained impassive, only handing out small praises. Janus was the best fighter of the group, though their stamina waned. Sollix was the slowest learner, but he fought energetically all day, flailing around the sand pit.

Mellia focused on keeping her magic light. She thought of saving her mother, hugging her, and going back to Palenque with her. Her Blazeguard spell stayed a light lilac color and did not return to the sulfuric smelling black tendrils of angry magic. Mellia hoped that when she was face to face with Heatheros, she could maintain sorcery of good. She did not admit it out loud, but her dark magic scared her.

At the end of training on the day before the crew was set to leave, Mellia's father shook hands with Sollix and Janus.

"Sollix, let Norma do more of the work. You swing her around like a wild animal, and she's not as effective," the admiral advised. "Janus, you're one of the best young fighters I've met. Don't forget to pace yourself. Your magic is powerful, and drains you quickly."

They nodded, and the admiral waved them off. When they were gone, he looked intensely at Mellia.

"You don't have to do this. I can intervene on your behalf with the Guild. We can figure something out."

Mellia's eyes flashed, and she felt her ring cutting into her closed fists. She answered in a tight voice, "Someone has to save Mom. Neathersby said there might be a clue."

Mellia couldn't understand why her father wouldn't do everything he could to save his lost wife. She looked at him, wishing he would respond and say he would come with her, or show her some magic this evening, just the two of them. *Or even just tell me he's proud of me,* she thought.

"I'm afraid I will lose you, too," Jonathan said, suddenly looking old and worn. His shoulders sagged, and he pulled his daughter into a soft and brief hug.

"Goodbye, Father," Melia said, turning to catch up with her friends.

"See you when you return. This isn't goodbye, Mellia," he answered, and he walked away in the opposite direction.

18

"No glorious send off?" Janus snickered, pulling their brown satchel back up to their shoulder.

"Did you miss the part about this being a secret mission?" Fret scolded. He was out of his silk pajamas and back in his sharp military greens.

The sun was just beginning to peek over the horizon, illuminating a tiny lugger boat with an impossibly small wooden overhang that appeared to be tight sleeping quarters. But it was better than snoozing on the minimal deck space around the weather-worn steel-wood masts.

Some dingy, water-stained sails hung limply on the masts. Mellia noticed the name "Adeline" painted in cursive in chipped blue paint. Biko roused himself from a nap in Mellia's coat pocket.

The Adeline bobbed in the water, roped to the dilapidated dock. Mellia stepped over a loose board, just avoiding a dip in the dark waters of the Loch. She put her satchel down, claiming the tiny bunk. She had at least expected a large glossy clipper with some preserve crests, proudly bearing the owl mascot, emblazoned on crisp white sails.

"Guess we are still roommates," Sollix said with a grin, breaking the trio's dismayed silence. He and Janus placed their satchels on either side of Mellia's sleeping mat.

"Say hello to Takeji if you find him," Fret said, and he saluted the young trio, spellaporting to his post at the gates of the zoo.

With Fret gone, the three stared at each other. None of them really knew how to sail. Sollix pulled out the map. As he rolled out the parchment, it seemed as if an invisible hand and plume were writing directions and little doodles on the map.

"Sing to her," the imperceptible hand scrawled.

"Sing to who?" Sollix asked, as if the map gave a perfectly rational response. The plume drew a rudimentary picture of the boat they were on.

"What shall we sing?" Sollix asked, beginning to warm up his voice by humming.

"Something in French. The language of love." The map answered by scratching out the letters as if it were obvious. Mellia thought the map was getting a bit snippy. Sollix sang the French version of the troll anthem.

At the close of the song, Sollix was trilling beautifully in a full falsetto. The rope attaching the tiny vessel to the ramshackle dock flipped off, and the misfit crew began their journey. Fueled by the serenade, the French boat tipped her bow towards Sollix, almost flirtatiously. Adeline ruffled her sails, as though she was a lady flipping her hair.

To see them off, Nessie jumped out of the water, nearly completing a clumsy backflip. Janus and Mellia waved. They would miss their morning visitor. They saluted Winston, the Guardgoyle, who was standing at attention on the wall. He saluted back, and Mellia swore she saw him wink at Nessie.

Before the tiny and inexperienced crew knew it, they had passed through the Caledonian Canal and could see the headwaters of the North Atlantic. The ocean was a plane of glass stretching endlessly before them. Still working on their sea legs, Mellia, Sollix, and Janus held each other's shoulders for balance as they traversed around the boat.

The day stretched into evening. Sollix alternated with twirling Norma's spiky ends towards the endless sea and arguing with the map. Apparently, Adeline navigated herself, as the map had drawn a bright blue line to an island. Mellia wasn't sure how this magic was working, but she knew the map and Adeline were working together.

Mellia worried for Biko. He was not meant for ocean travel. He had thrown up over the side. He couldn't hold down any water Mellia was able to give him. His light purple eyes were dull, his body almost lifeless. She gave him some herbs that helped with nausea, and the little monkey took some mixed with water and heated in Janus's pan.

Janus pulled a hanfu from their satchel and cast it in the water. Mellia could hear them mumbling some kind of paralysis spell. They pulled up the red fabric with three bright silver fish.

"Dinner is served!" they said excitedly, adding a small packet of rice and spices to the self-heating pan. They clubbed the fish on the side of the boat, much to Mellia's shock. She had never seen Janus do anything aggressive.

"I miss the Sammies," Sollix said, forking up a huge bite of fish and rice. Mellia was quiet, trying to feed Biko a bit of rice. After they ate, the group went to sleep on their skinny palettes. Mellia couldn't sleep and moved to sit in the front of the bow. Listening to Biko's heavy snores, she couldn't believe they were going back to the same grove where her mother had been kidnapped. She wondered what kinds of clues she could find.

The hours in the boat melted together. The keepers were restless. They had tried to discuss their mission plan, but they had no idea what to expect. Sollix's plan involved him incapacitating any poachers by attacking them with a Sanzembe Scream, as he was now calling his curdling yell, and taking them down with Norma. Eventually, Janus and Mellia gave him a look, and he was quiet. They watched the blue line representing the boat's journey on their map, slowly inching towards the rudimentary paint blob that the trio assumed was their destination.

The map scratched messages to Sollix about longitude and latitude, not swinging Norma while Adeline was traveling choppy waters, and how he was eating too much fish. Sollix pretended to be angry at the map, but Mellia could tell he enjoyed the attention. In fact, he seemed made for sailing.

On the fourth night, the crew was rounding the tip of Africa, and Mellia was taking her turn on watch. The night was warm, and the boat traveled languidly through the water as though it could feel the heat. With nowhere to go but the tiny deck, Mellia allowed herself to truly feel the deep ache of grief in her bones and her heart. Janus had told her to walk through her sorrow and not around it. Mellia was trying.

Mostly over his seasickness, Biko came to join her. He jumped lightly onto her shoulder and rested his soft head against the side of hers. Rather than try to soothe her heartache, she felt the little monkey grieving his losses, too. *How did it feel, Biko, when you saw the Satori at the Preserve?* Mellia questioned her companion with her thoughts.

Biko allowed Mellia to see his memories of the terrible day at the grove and of reuniting with some relatives at the preserve. But he let her see that his warmest and happiest memories were with her, eating pasta on her shoulder in the great hall, weaving flower crowns with their nimble fingers in Palenque, and snuggling together at night.

Lost in her emotions, the gnelf did not notice the large ripples on the port side, nor the oily trail that had appeared with the undulating water. A large creature followed the boat for several miles, knifing through the water silently. The Adeline suddenly stopped and lurched. Hard.

Janus was first to their feet. "Mellia, what's going on?" they said, instantly alert, bespelling a bright light onto the tip of their wand. The water around them was slick with black grease. Janus put their arms out for balance, whipping Scorchvine through the air and casting a bright, fiery light around the boat.

The tiny boat was trying to pull away from something, as if she was frightened. Janus pointed his makeshift torch towards the water. Mellia saw a serpentine figure's tail wrapped around the stern of the boat.

"Ikuchi!" she yelled, remembering Cavendish's guidebook.

Biko jumped deep into her robes, shivering. Sollix was up, looking angrily at slippery coils. He swung Norma bravely over his head, and she shot spikes that glanced off the sea monster's thick, armor-like scales.

Diving to the end of the deck, Sollix attempted to grasp at a section of water snake with all of his strength. His large hands slipped around, but he was able to dig his long, thick fingers under the monster's scales, and he gripped and pulled. He yelled, and a vein bulged on his forehead. Sweat beaded on his head, as he began to loosen the Ikuchi's hold.

Suddenly, the sea creature twisted its body, and its head rose above Sollix. Mellia remembered a drawing of the creature in her guidebook. Seeing its cold black eyes, slit nostrils, and piercing fangs caused her to freeze in fear. Like a striking snake, the Ikuchi lunged at Sollix, knocking him down with its blunt head. He flew back across the boat, and lay limply against the panels of the boat's bow.

Mellia cried out and tried to run to Sollix, but the boat was rocking and lurching, still trying to escape the attack. Biko bravely jumped from her pocket and went to tend to the unmoving troll.

"Firessence!" Janus yelled.

Their scepter pointed towards the Ikuchi. An arc of fire shot towards the sea beast, and the creature shrieked. Mellia could smell its cooking flesh, the scent of rot and burning oil. This seemed to enrage the animal more. Now in pain, the Ikuchi raised its tail and slapped the boat. Mellia heard boards snapping. Janus shot another incinerating flare towards their attacker. The Ikuchi dove under the water, dodging the blaze.

Unwilling to wait for the predator to strike again, Mellia dove into the water. She landed on the Ikuchi's back, just behind its neck. It flailed and thrashed its head to the side, trying to toss her off.

Numbed by the cold water, Mellia almost lost her grip. The Ikuchi whipped out of the water, and Mellia sucked in a huge breath, ready to submerge. Her heart pounded in her chest, and she tightened her legs around the animal's neck as it dove into the dark depths.

Clearing her mind, as the Satori had taught her, Mellia thought of everything at once, and then nothing. She felt herself connect with the Ikuchi, and she slipped into its mind. She manifested calming, food, swimming safely, and other things that she thought a sea monster might enjoy. She could read its memories and feel its pain.

She saw the Ikuchi as an infant water snake, caught in a net. The sea monster's mind flashed to being held in a dark tank. Mellia could see fuzzy figures above the tank sending Aferiora spells into the water, burning the Ikuchi through its plates.

She empathized with its fear and grief. Mellia strained to see who the figures were, and she realized she already knew. Lastly, she could feel a cold presence gripping the water snake's mind, forcing it to attack the boat. Mellia pushed against the force, and she felt it burst.

The Ikuchi seemed stunned, and it floated to the surface. Mellia gasped for air when she broke the plane of the water. She coughed and sputtered, still hanging onto the slimy serpent. The boat managed to drag itself to her, but one of the deck boards was cracked, and Mellia could see it was slowly taking on water. Sollix was still out cold, and Janus weakly pulled her into the vessel.

Janus was pale, and a rivulet of blood dripped from their nose. They slumped against the side of the boat. "Janus, what's wrong?" Mellia asked.

"I guess a Firessence spell really takes it out of you," they mumbled weakly, clutching Scorchvine to their chest. Mellia felt icy cold water soaking the bottom of her sodden robes. Mellia felt helpless. She herself was exhausted from melding with the creature, not to mention nearly drowning.

She saw another giant ripple in the water, and out sprung the head of an impossibly bigger Ikuchi. Its eyes glowed yellow and it raised itself up. Mellia could see the smaller Ikuchi coiled around its body. The sea creature stared intently at Mellia, and she waited for it to strike.

Well, at least I die with my three best friends, she thought, resigned to the fate of a watery grave. The giant Ikuchi dipped its head, and Mellia flinched, covering her head with her hands. She felt the boat moving forward. When she dared to open her eyes, the larger Ikuchi was gently pushing the boat with its head. Janus was staring with their mouth gaping.

Mellia felt no malevolence emanating from the creature, and suddenly she understood. This monster was the smaller Ikuchi's mother. Mellia placed her hand on the creature's snout. She felt its gratitude, and the creature showed her scenes of her baby being ripped from her by the large nets of the Darkentine Council.

The young sea creature had been taken and mind melded into a warrior. Mellia had destroyed the evil hypnospell that was holding the infant Ikuchi hostage.

As the enormous sea monster gently pushed the trio forward, Mellia tended to Sollix and the Ikuchi. Sollix had a giant cut on the side of his head where he had been struck. The area around the cut was swelling until Mellia applied a poultice with some uniceros paste. She used the rest of the salve to heal the Ikuchi's burned skin.

Biko jumped back into Mellia's pocket, and she could feel his overwhelm. Janus pulled another hanfu from their bag and shoved it into the crack of the boat's bottom. They used their pot to bail out some of the water the boat had taken on. The crew sat silently through the night, grateful to be alive and only slightly injured.

The broken ship struck shore at dawn. The exhausted mother Ikuchi had pushed the sinking wreck for miles. She bowed her giant head towards Mellia and swam back into dark depths. Just before they disappeared from view, Mellia saw the young sea snake jump out of the water, flipping in a happy salute.

Sollix was first to jump from the ship's broken frame into the waist deep water. Mellia's body was sore and covered with cuts and bruises. Her robes were torn and stained with serpent oil, and her hair was a greasy swath, matted to her head with the Ikuchi's oil. Biko shivered in her coat pocket, cold and shocked. His mind was unusually quiet. Sollix was spotted with large contusions, and though the cut on his scalp was closed, rivulets of dried blood stained his face. Even the usually perfectly coiffed Janus had torn robes and tangled hair. Their eyes were unusually wide with distress and exhaustion.

19

After resting, Sollix climbed a tree and brought down a bunch of coconuts. Janus used their scepter to burn perfectly elegant holes in the tops of the fruit so they could drink the clear, sweet water. Mellia secured Adeline on the shore. The boat seemed just as traumatized as its passengers, and her wood planks shivered in the sand.

As she returned to the group of logs and palm trees, she saw Janus neatly organizing their gear and creating a makeshift campsite. Out of the corner of her eye, she saw a thin, tall figure with orange bushy ears, a fluffy tail, and a white robe.

As the stranger approached, Janus raised Scorchvine in the air, manifesting a small but menacing crimson flame. Sollix enlarged Norma, twirling the morning star and accidentally hitting himself in the leg. Mellia realized the creature was half fox and half woman. The fox lady put her hands up and smiled a wide toothy grin.

"Whoa there!" she said in a warm tone, her voice low and scratchy. "I'm a friend." She took off the magic ring she wore and placed it gently in the sand next to her. "See, without my ring, I'm as powerless as a freshly born pup."

Mellia did not like how the red-haired woman licked her teeth when she said the words freshly and pup. Mellia reached out tele-pathically to Biko. *I can't read her,* he said, his voice tiny and weak from the shipwreck. *She's good and bad.* Mellia thought back, *Stay hidden and rest, little friend.*

"I'm Kitsune. My friends call me Kitsu. I'm a longtime friend of Neathersby, that cranky old bag. She sent a letter, through a particularly handsome mermaid, announcing your arrival. I've been waiting for you."

Kitsune laughed a little too loudly at her own joke at Neathersby's expense, and her smile was a bit too big and, well, foxlike. The crew still looked dumbfounded at the red canine-woman that stood before them.

She stuck out her hand in introduction, and her nails were filed to a point. Her arms and hands were covered in light orange hair. Still cautious, neither Janus nor Sollix lowered their weapons. However, Mellia reached her hand out and shook her paw, slipping into Kitsune's thoughts.

Her mind was a jumble of painful memories and indecision. Mellia grasped a specific memory of a Darkentine wizard spella-porting into her ramshackle thatched beach hut. Mellia felt Kitsune's terror as the evil stranger pointed his wand towards her face and burned a gash in her chin. Mellia could see the wizard speaking, and she could hear garbled arguing.

Kitsune ripped her pawish hand out of Mellia's grip. She bared her teeth and growled at the gnelf. Sollix stepped between the two.

"Watch it, Fox," Sollix snarled, raising Norma up into the air.

"Sollix, don't. She's a Yokai. And that pearl on her tail is how we will find Takeji," Mellia said, stopping her friend's attack.

Mellia could almost hear her mother's voice reading from magibiologist Sakuma Toshiko's *Guide to Island Spirits*. She remembered now that Yokai were spirits that inhabited the island of Oshima, and they were known to be both benevolent and deadly, depending on their mood. She also remembered that in order to get the fox woman's help, they would need to steal the jewel from her tail.

"I say we just take it," Sollix snapped, surly with hunger and exhaustion. Kitsune grabbed her tail and the pearl in mock fear.

"My pearl?" Kitsune edged slightly away from the troll. "Well, I have been kind of lonely and bored on this beach, so I'll give you a riddle. If you solve the riddle, I will loan you my pearl. You don't even have to steal it. One-time special deal. I can be your guide to find Takeji. It will be dangerous--the Darkentine Council has been all over lately. Deal?"

The trio looked at each other. Not seeing many other options, Mellia nodded in agreement. Kitsune picked her ring up from the sand and slipped it back on her pointer finger.

"Here's the riddle: I have rivers, but don't have water. I have dense forests, but no trees and animals. I have cities, but no people live in those cities. What am I?" Kitsune queried.

"How many guesses do we get?" Sollix asked, looking revived. He loved a puzzle.

"Hmm..." Kitsune thought. "How about three?" she said with a smile.

20

The trio returned to the cluster of palm trees, where Janus had made a temporary camp. The fox went back inside her hut down the beach, and they hoped they were out of earshot.

"I don't trust that fox person," Janus said between large gulps of StreamDeep's refreshing supply. "Something isn't right there. Remember what Neathersby was telling Fret...she told no one about the mission. The fox lies."

"I think we need her as a guide," Mellia countered. "We barely survived the Ikuchi attack; who knows what else is out there? This is life and death...think about what happened to my mother."

Mellia and Janus looked at Sollix to make the decision.

"Let's solve the riddle and see what happens. We can always ditch the fox. Three of us, one of her," Sollix decided.

In agreement, the three began to analyze parts of the riddle. "It couldn't be a desert," Janus said, thinking aloud. The others nodded.

"Or an old abandoned castle with a moat," Sollix mumbled, brainstorming.

The rolled map in Sollix's bag rustled, trying to escape. He pushed it back down. The three continued trying to solve the riddle.

They guessed an underwater city, a tree with owls, and many other incorrect answers. The map had been frustratingly trying to get out of Sollix's satchel. Finally, it leapt in the air and smacked him in the head.

"That's it!" Janus exclaimed. "It's a map."

Kitsune appeared out of nowhere, sitting on a log next to Mellia as though she had been there the whole time.

"Took you long enough. I gave you an easy one. I need some adventure," she stated with a smirk on her thin, black lips, her yellow eyes glinting. She removed the pearl from her tail and placed it in Mellia's hand. "Keep this safe; I'll be needing it back."

Mellia held Kitsune's pawlike hand as they made the exchange. She tried to enter her mind, but she only saw an endlessly tall and long black wall.

"Not this time, gnelf--a lady has to have some secrets." Kitsune's throat rumbled as she firmly pulled her fingers from Mellia's grasp. "We leave in the morning."

With that, she disappeared again. Sollix began dragging logs, building a lean-to shelter for the night. Janus took a hanfu from their bag and waded out into the pristine blue of the ocean to fish. Mellia gathered soft fronds and began to weave them into loose sleeping mats.

The three laid down after a giant meal of flame-roasted tuna that was flaky and buttery. Janus paired the fish with some island mushrooms Mellia scavenged when looking for palm fronds for their rudimentary shelter. She was almost completely sure the fungi was edible. It reminded her of the kind she would scavenge with her grandfather in Palenque.

After dinner, night fell. Mellia felt tense. She didn't know if she could trust Kitsune, and she ruminated on how easily the map riddle was solved.

Something felt wrong. She didn't know who she would meet from the Darkentine Council, and if her mother and father had failed at their mission, how could she possibly win? Biko felt her worry and shared his own. This was the place where his whole family was nearly slaughtered. From her time with the Satori, Mellia remembered seeing a flash of red disappearing into the bushes the day her mother was kidnapped. *Could that have been Kitsune? Had she fled the scene?* Mellia wondered.

The trio lay under the shelter, staring through the slats in the roof at the stars. The group was unusually quiet that evening, though not one of them slept easily. Instead of Sollix's usual booming snores, he flipped and turned, causing the lean-to beams to wobble. Finally, Mellia fell into a fitful sleep.

21

Mellia woke up, startled, with a hand on her shoulder. A serious-looking Kitsune motioned for her to get up. Sollix and Janus were already packing their robes. They destroyed what was left standing of the tiny refuge, shouldered their bags, and began walking down the beach. Mellia noticed Kitsune had a satchel of her own, along with a large, silver machete slung in a belt. Kitsune led them off the beach into the forest. The trail she chose was thin, and almost disappeared in parts. Compared to the open expanse of the island beach, Mellia felt constricted by the wooded cluster of trees. The canopy blocked out much of the morning sunlight, and everything was bathed in green hues.

The trees were covered in emerald moss, and verdant leaves carpeted the ground. The air was thick and cloying, and even with the short distance the group had covered, Mellia felt out of breath and choked. With Kitsune so far ahead, Sollix growled and pulled out his map.

It unrolled impatiently, and instead of a glowing blue line running to the island, there was now a bright green track weaving through rudimentary images of trees and up a mountain. A bright red "X" was stamped in its center, surrounded by lined sketches of Takeji, the cranes, the pond, and cherry blossom trees.

"Put the map away, Troll--you don't need it. The gnelf has my pearl. That means I have to guide you to Takeji, whether I like it or not." Kitsune called, still keeping just within the eyesight of the trio.

Sollix rolled his eyes and tucked the map back in his bag. He swung Norma around as though he was bushwhacking branches, but most of the tree limbs whipped back perilously into his face.

As the group moved deeper into the forest, Mellia tried to distract herself from her claustrophobic feelings by focusing on her surroundings. The forest, though crowded with flora, was beautiful. It seemed to breathe on its own.

Birds of all colors dotted the dark tangles of branches, and Mellia noticed a particular bird with a long flowing tail, shining like blue and purple jewels. Tiny little white birds chittered excitedly with each other and seemed to follow the group.

Large bugs crawled on logs, and Kitsune occasionally bent down and snatched grubs and beetles, popping them into her mouth and crunching loudly as she walked.

"You'll never go hungry in these woods," she remarked, looking back at the group, a beetle's long, serrated bug leg hanging from her mouth. Mellia wondered if she would get hungry enough to eat insects. She hoped not.

When it became almost too dark to see their own feet without wandlight, Janus waved his hand over Scorchvine, and the scepter glowed a violent red. Kitsune hissed for him to put it out.

"Darkentine poachers," she hissed. "We will have to stop here tonight--it's too dark to continue."

They were near a stream, and Mellia filled the StreamDeep flask. Janus rolled their eyes when Mellia shared some water with Kitsune. Mellia noticed they had been watching the fox woman closely all day.

Kitsune pulled a blow dart gun from her bag. She skillfully put it to her lips and tucked a dart in. She shot into the darkness, and a thick white snake thudded to the ground. Kitsune had sent the dart clean through its eye and into its brain. Its wide body writhed and slowly stilled.

"Dinner!" she exclaimed, sounding accomplished. Janus built a small fire but refused to eat any of the fallen reptile. Sollix exclaimed that he liked the snakey flavor, saying it tasted like a jungle chicken.

Mellia peeled off the skin and let the chewy snake meat slide down her throat. She tried to avoid tasting and chewing as much as possible, but she knew she needed sustenance. Biko jumped out of her pocket and darted into the darkness.

Before Mellia could panic over the missing monkey, he brought back some berries and stalks of a plant that looked a lot like celery. He sat on Janus's shoulder and shared his vegetarian stash with the hungry wizard.

During the meal, Mellia marveled at the animated Yokai's story-telling prowess. Using wild gestures, voices, and accents, Kitsune told the story of the Battle of White Beach.

"The sun made the white sand sparkle like endless stars," Kitsune began.

"I was on the beach that morning gathering moon shells for a necklace for the chief of our tribe. I paused to snatch a sand crab for a snack when I saw pure darkness coming down the beach."

The Yokai shivered visibly but continued.

"I counted ten Darkentine Poachers coming towards our village. They radiated evil, and I could feel it from across the beach. Dark grey storm clouds followed, and their deep red robes whipped around. Their hoods blew back, revealing grey, scarred faces. I shrunk against the rock, not daring to peek out.

"I was relieved to hear Saito's voice speaking for the tribe. His voice sounded so brave rising above the waves. 'You have no business here.' Saito growled towards the intruders. I dared to look, and I saw Saito flanked by the most skilled warriors in the tribe.

"'Just show us to the cranes, and we will spare your life,' the leader of the poachers hissed, squinting in the bright sun. The poachers drew their wands threateningly, and menacing black sparks spit from the end.

"'Attack,' Saito yelled. In a flash of shelled armor, the Yokai transformed themselves into gigantic demons with twisted faces, huge fangs, and spiked tails. Saito leapt into the air towards the leader.

"'You're mine, Heatheros!' Saito shouted, firing malevolent dark blue streaks of magic towards the poacher. Saito wounded Heatheros, leaving his arm bleeding and his robe smoking. The poacher put up a black shield made from writhing black threads of magic. Saito's blasts were absorbed by the shield, and it grew larger.

"Heatheros reached out from behind his shield and shot at Saito. Saito quickly deflected the blast, and it ricocheted, slicing down a nearby palm tree. Tetsuni Ishida threw balls of fire from her hands and mouth toward the advancing group of poachers. The attackers hid behind the shield, and the Yokai magic was soaked into the bulwark as it continued to expand to protect the poachers.

"Tetsuni bowed towards Saito. Before he could protest, Tetsuni vaulted into the air over the poachers as Saito began firing rapidly towards the poachers to distract them. He avoided the shield, as he understood the blasts were reinforcing the evil magic. Tetsuni roared fire into the poachers, and I dared to feel hopeful as five fell at once, charred and bleeding. Victor flipped the shield towards the enraged demon and shot her directly in the chest. The black tendrils stuck to her and buried themselves under her skin.

"Tetsuni cried out and then lay still on the ground, transformed back to her slight fox woman frame in death. Saito and the other warriors were able to strike three more of the poachers. Heatheros flipped the shield back toward the Yokai.

"Heatheros growled an otherworldly howl and levitated himself above the battling Yokai and poachers. He cast a black flame over the Yokai while his warriors huddled under the shield. I slid down behind my rock. I watched as the flame seemed to burn over the sand towards my village."

Kitsune stopped her story there, unable to continue. Mellia pitied the mischievous fox, who had lost everything at the hands of the poachers. Sollix pretended he wasn't crying. Even Janus wiped a tear.

"Your people fought bravely," Janus said.

Mellia felt herself relax and trust the fox creature a bit more. Surely Kitsune wouldn't double cross them to help the same people that had torn apart her peaceful village. She noticed Janus seemed to unwind, laying their scepter in their lap instead of keeping it ready to strike.

Janus offered to take the first watch so the others could rest. It had been a long day trudging through the steamy jungle. Mellia felt the chill in the night air, and listened to the grunts, howls, and squeaks of nocturnal creatures. Mellia thought she could see several pairs of glowing eyes watching their camp. She convinced herself she was being paranoid.

Biko hopped from the makeshift leaves Mellia had piled into a bed and sat with Janus. She could hear Janus talking softly and soothingly to the monkey. Sollix snored loudly, and Kitsune joked that the sound would keep any predators away. In the deepest and darkest part of the night, Mellia felt Janus' soft touch rousing her awake.

"Your turn to take watch," they whispered, trying not to disturb the sleeping adventurers. "Do you want me to cast some wandlight?"

"No, it's okay, I got it," Mellia said, rousing herself. She had her own wand and was able to produce a sputtering glow, which was nothing in comparison to Janus' bright, unwavering crimson light. The wizard lay down where Mellia was, and they fell asleep right away.

Kitsune joined Mellia in the darkness. With a bit of magic, Kitsune made a tiny fire and placed a dented tin mug over it. Without much light, Mellia couldn't see what the Yokai was mixing into the mug. She handed Mellia the steaming mug, full to the brim with hot liquid.

"Some tea," Kitsune said. "It will help keep you awake."

"Thank you," said the gnelf gently. "My mother used to make me tea at night." Mellia told Kitsune some stories about her mother dressing up for Dia De Los Muertos and taking her to Chiapas to celebrate. The gnelf slowly trailed off in the middle of the story, and Kitsune gently laid her down, as she had fallen fast asleep.

22

old water seeped into Mellia's mouth, nose, and eyes, jerking Mellia awake. Her head pounded painfully, and the sun through the forest canopy made white pinpricks in her eyes. Sollix and Janus's faces floated over her, expressions pinched with concern.

"I'm fine, except for this headache," Mellia rasped. "Shouldn't we get going?" she added, shaking leaves from her hair and wondering why she felt slightly dizzy.

"We would if we knew where to go," Sollix said glumly. Mellia felt for the pearl in her pocket, but the tiny iridescent ball was gone.

"The map's gone, too," Janus added, as if they were reading Mellia's next thought. "Along with my scepter."

"We've been outfoxed," Sollix said in an uncharacteristically sarcastic tone, handing Mellia the StreamDeep bottle. Sollix waved Norma around limply. "She left Norma, though."

Mellia's ring still glinted on her finger. She thought it was odd that the fox hadn't removed it, as it was very valuable.

Kitsune had left the metal cup behind, and Janus showed Mellia the remaining herbs sticking to the bottom. Mellia tasted the soggy leaves. "Valerian root and passion flower, disguised with lemon peels," she analyzed. "Clever."

Sollix kicked a log that splintered into small pieces.

"We're lost. We'll die in this jungle. Fret was right; we weren't made for this. We were outsmarted by a fox, and we didn't even come close to Takeji. Mellia! Why did you drink that tea?" Sollix's voice had risen to a yell.

Mellia felt tendrils of anger curling inside. "Well, if you hadn't been snoring like some kind of congested Elegon, you could have sat watch with me."

Both of their eyes were blazing with fury, and they stood face to face. Mellia looked to Janus for help, but they averted their eyes.

"Lazy troll," Mellia spat.

"Whiny gnelf," Sollix looked at her for the first time with disdain.

Biko hopped on Mellia's shoulder. He placed his tiny hand on Mellia's cheek and stretched his tail to brush it against Sollix's face. Biko showed them memories of laughing in the banquet hall and giggling about Jayadeva Bhakta, the Owltender. He flashbacked to Mellia taking desserts for Sollix, and him teasing her because she couldn't spellaport.

With the help of the tiny Satori, Mellia and Sollix could not stay angry. Sollix wrapped Mellia into a suffocating hug, and just as quickly as the argument started, it ended.

As Sollix released Mellia from a bone crunching embrace, Mellia felt a heavy drop hit her shoulder. She looked, and one of the strange white birds she had seen, during their trudge through the jungle, had defecated on her shoulder.

"Gross bird! Kick me while I'm down," she shouted at the flock of oblivious fowl. Biko jumped to the top of Sollix's head, screaming with excitement.

He pointed at the birds frantically. Mellia put her forearm out, and Biko leapt onto it, grasping her hand. In their minds, he showed Mellia the birds flying through the forest and up Mount Yoshino to where the cherry grove stood. In the grove sat an unharmed Takeji, with a safe and unbothered flock of cranes.

"Ah...I see it now. Well done, Biko!" Mellia squealed, squeezing the smart little monkey in her arms.

Sollix and Janus looked confused. "Follow the birds!" Mellia said. Biko says they come to the forest to scavenge for sweet Ume berries to feed their babies, who nest in the groves of the cherry glens on the mountain. They can lead us out."

Biko nodded and climbed up the tree. He chattered rapidly, waving his hands at the birds for several minutes. He went to a bush and began to gather some tiny Ume berries on a bush under the birds. He motioned for his friends to do the same. The birds chirped and fluttered their wings excitedly.

They packed their satchels with as much fruit as they could carry. The tightknit bunch of tiny white birds began to fly, stopping to wait for their unwinged plum couriers to catch up.

23

Biko had done it. The birds led them to the edge of the forest just before nightfall. The tree line stopped abruptly, revealing the enormous spread of a mountain in front of them. It seemed to climb into the sky, and the top was blanketed in thick white clouds. Its base was wide and rocky, and much of the mountain was a flat, sheer face that Mellia wondered how they would ascend.

Outside of the moist, fetid forest air, Mellia welcomed the openness of the rocky outcropping that skirted the bluffs before them. The birds began to fly towards the rocks. Feeling invigorated and closer to their goal than ever before, the ragtag cluster of adventurers began to jog.

They reached the dark gray sheer cliffs as the sun drooped over the horizon, and the birds tucked themselves into wind-worn pockets in the rock. Mellia could see them cuddling for warmth and knew they were signaling it was time to stop for the night.

Biko showed Mellia an image of a cave just a short walk ahead. The little monkey found it easily, and Sollix threw some boulders that were blocking the entrance off to the side. Janus produced some dried mushrooms from their bag and made a tiny fire for their friends. They snuck a few of the plums from Mellia's satchel and roasted them on sticks they found on the cave floor.

"These aren't half bad," Sollix commented, grabbing more mushrooms from Janus's pouch and stabbing his stick through their meaty core.

That night, Mellia and Sollix sat watch at the mouth of the cave. Huddled together for warmth, Mellia envied the little white birds, who had plumped their feathers up for heat.

Sollix spoke about his family. He talked about how his father was a fierce warrior who had wanted Sollix to join the Warriors Academy with his three older brothers. Sollix did not get into the academy because he wasn't as brutally strong. His brothers called him "Sweet Baby Troll." After failing the trials for the Warrior's Academy, Sollix had returned to the village so his parents could decide his next path. In the dinner tent, his cousins and younger brothers would elbow him and steal his meat. He ignored the bullying and savage treatment by his own family members. He pretended not to notice the disappointed gazes of the village elders piercing him.

Sollix eventually met another troll that had also failed to enter the Warrior's Academy. His name was Yavo, and his father was one of the village shamans. He was going to be sent to the Healing School, run by gnomes. Shunned by their kin, Yavo and Sollix began to spend a lot of time together.

Each morning, the two would head to a well outside of the village to collect water. They eventually developed feelings and shared a kiss near the deep shaft spring, thinking no one else saw. Yavo's little sister had been sent by his parents to watch Yavo, as they were suspicious of him and Sollix.

Yavo's sister told the entire village what she had seen. Yavo was sent to the Healing School. "And that's how I ended up at the preserve." Sollix ended his story, sadness in his warm wide eyes.

"Sollix, you are better than them. They might have brute strength, but you have a loyal and brave heart, and that makes you a true warrior."

"Thank you, friend," Sollix said, squeezing her hand. Mellia could see in his mind at that moment that she could trust him and Janus. There was nothing but feelings of loyalty, friendship, and love.

Mellia smiled. "Also, there are no gooey chocolate brownies--and definitely no Jayadeva--at the Warriors Academy," she said, nudging Sollix with her elbow.

The morning sunrise streaked the sky behind the mountain with pinks, oranges, and gold. Janus and Biko had finished off the night watch and were dispersing the small fire coals. The birds were flitting around the group in the sky. They set off after the birds, following a vague and rocky trail of switchbacks that climbed up the sheer mountain face.

Janus gracefully glided up the trail while Sollix's large feet slipped dangerously off the side, knocking pebbles and detritus off the side. Mellia tried not to watch the rocks falling longer and longer distances until she could not hear them hit the ground.

The crew climbed through the night, as the quarter moon and Janus's wand provided enough light. They could see the summit straight above them and could not stop to rest with such little space on the trail. StreamDeep was empty, and the crew was feeling the effects of the high altitude and dehydration.

As a troll, Sollix had not experienced such high altitudes. His pace was slowing, and Mellia stayed with him. Mellia noticed her friend walking unevenly and weaving dangerously on the narrow mountain trail.

Sollix began to sway. He tipped off the side, falling, and was lost in the thick morning mist. Norma loosed from his coat and dropped into the mist as well. Mellia lurched forward, trying to grab him. She saw a spray of pebbles from the trail, saw the white abyss before her, and thought she would join her friend in falling to her death.

She felt a slight tug on her robe, and Biko managed to pull the end of her robe, balancing her so she was no longer leaning off the trail.

"Janus! He fell!" Mellia screamed. Ripping off their satchel and tossing it to Mellia, Janus did not hesitate. They jumped from the cliff, diving down into the fog where Sollix had tumbled toward the earth. Mellia wrung her hands, but Biko smiled and pointed.

Rising through the fog was a bright red, scaly snout. Then the tips of some equally crimson wings sliced through the mist. Mellia could not believe her eyes. She closed and reopened them a few times as the dragon floated above where Mellia stood. *It's a dragon and it's Janus,* she thought. *Janus is a dragon!*

Janus glided over to the ledge, and Mellia and Biko hopped onto their back. Even as a dragon, Janus was beautiful. Their scales were a deep red, spotted with gold and black plates. Their eyes were a luminescent brown, slitted with a black pupil. Their wings were long and slender, just like Janus's own arms.

Their long, black-tipped tail swayed behind them as Janus flew up to the summit, and their legs were tucked gracefully under their slender chest and belly.

"So, why didn't you lead with this?" Mellia asked.

"It's supposed to be a secret," they answered. Mellia startled a bit at Janus's smooth voice, expecting a raspy, reptilian growl.

"Secret's out," Mellia mumbled. Sollix was hanging onto Janus, but his eyes were closed and his skin was absent of color.

"We need to get him some water," Mellia said, tending to Sollix since her shock had somewhat worn off.

Janus nodded and flapped their wings harder towards the summit of the mountain. Janus hovered at the ledge, and Mellia pulled Sollix down.

Mellia dipped the SpringDeep flask into the mud and was able to fill it. The water turned clear, and she held the bottle to Sollix's lips. He sputtered, but then he grasped the bottle and took some heavy gulps. Mellia refilled it three times before the troll was sated. He was able to sit up but was woozy.

Janus's normally sharp eyes were dull and listless. Janus collapsed next to Sollix and the two passed the SpringDeep back and forth. They leaned against a large rock some distance from the summit's edge.

"Now what?" Janus grumbled, slightly rejuvenated. "We have no map and no food, and we can barely walk. I say we wait here until morning and then head back."

Mellia looked to Sollix for support. She felt that they should continue forward. Mellia could not fail. But Sollix shook his head weakly.

Mellia prepared a pep talk in her head, but before she could get the words out, she heard a deep, rumbling growl.

24

Two of the strangest creatures the trio had ever seen rolled out in a ball of red, white, and orange fur, from a cluster of bushes onto rocky ground near the stone where Sollix and Janus rested. They were hissing and biting, batting each other like playful kittens.

Definitely not kitten-sized, the beasts were leonine in nature, with heavy brows looming over two pairs of bronze-colored eyes. Giant platinum manes framed their faces, connecting to long strands of curled mustaches, jutting from the creatures' jowls. Rows of sharp jadestone teeth glinted in the late afternoon sun.

Mellia thought Sollix and Janus looked like easy prey. Sensing their presence, the cats pulled apart. Playfulness gone, the beasts gracefully padded forward, and the gnelf realized how large the predators were. She figured Sollix standing his tallest reached their chest height. Their hind legs were pure muscle, and sharpened jade stone claws protruded from their feet.

The creatures prowled towards the stricken troll and Gaiden. Biko tried to distract the predators by jumping into a nearby tree and chattering with all his might. Focused on their larger prey, the cats slunk towards Sollix and Janus.

Realizing the beasts hadn't seen her, Mellia crept up silently behind them. She needed a solid grip on one of their tails to enter their minds and distract them away. Just as she felt the soft, silken fur of one of the cats' hindquarters, it whipped its muscular tail around, knocking her through the air.

Mellia reeled backwards, her arms flailing, as she tried to grasp for anything solid. She hit the ground hard, still skidding across the smooth rock to the edge of the cliff. Mellia's feet kicked air, and she made one last effort to jam her fingers in wide cracks of the stone slabs. Her hand caught onto a crevice, and her shoulder tore slightly with the hanging weight of her lower body.

Mellia watched helplessly as the larger of the two beasts licked its lips. Just when the predators were a claws' swipe away, Janus wove his hands, pointing them towards the creatures while whispering a fire spell. Their fingers spat out a few flames, causing the leonine animals to take pause. Janus was too weak to summon enough fire to deter the giant cats.

The oversized feline creatures roared ferociously, and Janus' hair flew back, coating them in saliva that stank of rotted meat. The smaller of the two beasts swiped at Sollix with its meaty paw, leaving four straight gashes in the top of his arm. Sollix yelped in pain, clutching his arm to his chest.

He pushed at the giant paws and kicked at the cat's chest. Almost as if they were playing, the lions swatted at Sollix. Struggling to pull herself up, and try again to save her friends, Mellia saw a flash of reddish orange.

Kitsune's pointed face loomed above hers. With surprising strength for her thin frame, Kitsune grabbed Mellia's upper arms and pulled her over the ledge. Once the gnelf was on solid ground, Kitsune waggled her paws, and manifested a gigantic ball of thick red yarn.

"Here, kitty, kitty," Kitsune shouted in a high-pitched voice towards the cats. Instantly distracted, the large cats skittered and pounced around the end of the string Kitsune was dragging away from Sollix and Janus.

Mellia scrambled over to her friends. She winced at the red gashes across Sollix's arm and Janus' chest. The slash marks were flecked with jade crystals, and black, veiny lines of infection spread from the wound sites.

Meanwhile, Kitsune danced around the wide ledge as though she was cavorting with the ferocious beasts. She skipped and leapt, dragging the string behind her. The large cats rolled and jumped through the air, forgetting the hunt.

As she skipped around, Kitsune cast a spell, and several bear-sized mice made of light ran into the bushes. The feline duo foolishly jumped into the bushes, chasing the holographic rodents.

"Komainu," Kitsune explained with a shrug, as though two thirds of their group hadn't just been mauled. "Japanese guardian lions. You're getting closer to…"

"You!" Sollix roared at the fox woman, cutting her off. Sollix cracked his knuckles and squeezed his fists. Mellia had never seen him so enraged. His face was crimson, and blue veins bulged from his forehead. He raised the fist on his uninjured arm and charged at her. "You almost cost us our lives," he bellowed, then clutched his chest, heaving in pain.

25

Kitsune fell to her knees in surrender. She pulled Scorchvine from inside her gi, and handed it to them.

"You speak the truth, young Sollix," she said in an earnest whisper. "I'm here to make it right."

Janus and Mellia stood behind Sollix, who loomed over the prostrate fox woman.

"Why should we trust you?" Janus asked.

"You shouldn't," the fox replied. "But the map is gone, and the birds have flown on. I can still feel a Darkentine presence here."

"Why did you betray us?" Mellia questioned.

Still kneeling in deference, Kitsune sucked in a deep troubled breath. "Victor Heatheros. You've heard of him by now."

"He took my mother," Mellia said in a low and serious tone. Biko climbed up to Mellia's shoulder and shrieked at Kitsune, trying to explain his own tragedy.

Kitsune rose to her full height and motioned for the monkey to quiet. "I was there in the grove when your mother was kidnapped, Mellia. Biko, I saw many of your family suffer grave injury and even death. You see, gnelf, your parents also used me as a guide. They arrived shortly after Heatheros burned the village. They found me curled up in a pile of ashes, mourning, wishing for death. She told me stories all about you," Kitsune said with a tiny sad smile.

"Your mother spent several days nursing me back to health. She fed me soup and cleaned my soiled clothing. She brought me back to life. Your father hunted the three surviving poachers, to no avail."

"So how did they end up in the grove? It must be hard to find," Janus asked. Mellia stared at the fox woman, listening intently to Kitsune's every word.

"Very difficult, but not impossible," Kitsune admitted. "I agreed to guide your parents to the grove to protect the cranes, but I also hoped your father would kill Heatheros. When we arrived, I saw the slain Satori and fled."

Without noticing, Mellia began moving her hands through the air. Black swirls of dark magic curled between her fingers. She was breathing rapidly, and she felt a scream inside of her wanting to escape.

Biko calmed her with his mind, and Janus placed their hands over hers. The malignant coils dissipated, but not before Kitsune and Sollix noticed.

"Coward," Mellia spat.

"Let her continue," Janus said diplomatically, still holding Mellia's hands.

"Victor came back a few nights ago. He entered my hut in a cloak of darkness. He threatened me, warning me that a trio of young keepers would arrive on the island. He told me I needed to do away with you. He burned me with dark magic as warning of what could happen if I refused," Kitsune explained, rubbing the scar on her chin.

"I didn't know what to do," Kitsune explained, her voice wavering. "I was afraid of what Heatheros would do to you if you made it to the cranes and he was there. So I gave Mellia a sleeping draught and made off with the map--and my pearl."

Kitsune grabbed her tail and pulled it close. She stroked it. Mellia noticed the pearl was reattached, dangling from the tip on a magical filament. The fox woman gave the gem a tug and pulled it off. She placed it in Mellia's hand for the second time.

"There. Now I am bound to guide you. I will not steal it back. You must give it to me when you are ready. I swear this oath on the great and fallen Saito." Mellia held Kitsune's paw, checking the fox's mind.

"She's telling the truth...for once," stated the young gnelf, watching the fox closely with narrowed eyes. Kitsune quietly returned the map and scepter to their irked owners. Mellia slowed her rapid breathing. *Kitsune has suffered loss at the hands of Heatheros, too. Though she is devious, she's not my enemy,* Mellia thought. Biko sent her a mental message of agreement.

"I hope we do run into Heatheros; I'll kill him myself," the little gnelf threatened. Lifebender's white opalescence grew blindingly bright, responding to Mellia's promise to end the poacher's life. "Good to see Lifebender awake...maybe it will prove useful after all," she added.

Kitsune and Mellia made a makeshift camp at the edge of the forest, far from the edge of the cliffs. Mellia was able to forage some more mushrooms, and Kitsune caught a small rabbit. The exhausted group ate chunks of rabbit meat and fleshy brown mushrooms roasted on long sticks. Janus would not eat the rabbit, so Mellia gave him the largest toadstool cap.

After they ate and drank, Mellia retrieved the last of Janus's hanfus from their bag. By now, the Gaiden magic had worn off, and the golden dragons lay still on the garment.

She ripped it into pieces, balling some up and wetting it with water from StreamDeep. She tried to swab the angry red welts on Sollix's arm and Janus's chest. Green jade crystals crusted the sides of the gashes, sticking to their skin as Mellia tried in vain to clean the wounds. Sollix cried out in pain.

"Shh...you'll attract the Komainu--and predators far worse," Kitsune hissed at the moaning troll.

"Well, at least they left my good arm alone," Sollix said as Mellia put his left arm in a makeshift sling.

The wind blew heavily that night, slicing through the trees and chilling the group to the bone. They shivered all night, teeth clacking violently. Mellia noticed that Janus still kept their eyes on Kitsune.

Mellia worried most about Biko. He would only eat a few insects and leaves throughout the day and slept the rest of the time. She knew he was weakened by the difficult journey, but the closer he got to the magic cherry glen, the more wistful he became.

In the morning, the group chewed on some miner's lettuce Mellia found at the forest entrance. As he gnawed crabbily on the bitter-tasting leaves, Sollix's stomach bellowed.

"When we get back, I'm going to polish off the lot of Sammies," he grumbled, rubbing his hollow stomach with his good arm, as if that would ease his hunger.

Kitsune found some mucousy snails with bright yellow shells and thick, squishy bodies. Even Janus popped a few snails, swallowing them whole and then gagging. Sollix nodded his approval.

"Thanks, fox woman-- tastes like a dwarf's sneeze. But not bad," he critiqued.

"You're welcome, Troll. We have arrived at the grove."

26

Crossing through a tight knot of **trees**, the cherry blossom grove splayed before the weary travelers. Despite the prior mayhem, the sweet-smelling blossoms spread over the top of the grove. The pond in the center was clean and clear, somehow washed clean of Satori blood.

With Kitsune at her side, and Janus and Sollix laboring to keep up, Mellia paused, taking in the scene before her. Biko shivered in her pocket, unmoving. Mellia could feel his tormented thoughts.

An old man knelt across the pond. Several of the origami cranes flitted towards him. Even from far away, Mellia saw the written spells, ancient calligraphy hovering just over the intricate paper feathers. The old man giggled and chatted with the cranes, as though it was normal to be doing so. He paused and grinned at a tiny paper bird with the few teeth he had left.

Even though the old wizard was acting ridiculously, Mellia sensed his primitive and powerful magic. Though it was invisible, there was an aura of protective energy around Takeji. *That's why Neathersby said he could handle himself*, she thought.

As though he had just realized there were newcomers, Takeji

stood up. Mellia incorrectly assumed the old man would hunch over and struggle to walk. Takeji stood stick straight, and out of nowhere, he jumped in the air and clicked his heels together. He pointed at Mellia and bent his long, bony fingers, indicating she should approach. Janus and Sollix settled on a log nearby, looking relieved to be resting. Kitsune's ears flicked, and her eyes darted around the perimeter of the grove, preparing for danger.

Mellia looked questioningly at her friends, and Janus nodded for her to proceed. Biko slipped out of her pocket. Mellia walked cautiously over to the old man. When they reached the other side of the pond, Biko jumped from her shoulder. He landed on Takeji's outstretched arm, and the two put their foreheads together.

Biko cooed, grunted, and howled, and Mellia figured out he was relaying the perils of their journey. When Biko finished, Takeji petted the monkey on the head. Despite his age, Takeji's warm brown eyes sparkled like a child's. He wordlessly held out his hand to Mellia. She took it, marveling at the papery smoothness of his skin.

He opened his mind to her, sharing hundreds of years of memories. Mellia was reminded of a huge hardbound book, where each fast-turning page was a memory of Takeji's. When he reached the end, close to the present, Mellia saw the scene from the Satori.

In Takeji's memory, it was moments before her mother's kidnapping in the grove. He had made himself and his cranes invisible. He sat huddled with his dozen shivering origami birds, undetectable to anyone, as Victor slaughtered and maimed the Satori. When she saw Takeji's memory of her father entering the grove, she threw Takeji's hand down, breaking their mental communication.

Mellia lost control of her constantly simmering anger. The dark ball of rage and grief for her mother opened. She felt the fury at her father, at Kitsune, and now Takeji. All of them could have helped, could have intervened.

Her hands massaged the air, and Lifebender gleamed like a beacon passing through the air. She screamed, "You could have saved her! You did nothing!" She raised her hands to strike Takeji with her ill-intentioned Blazeguard, wanting someone to hurt like she hurt on the inside.

The old man closed his eyes and turned up his palms in acceptance of the gnelf's furious spell. Before Mellia could fling the black fiber towards the wizard, she heard a terrified shout tear from Kitsune's throat.

27

Her concentration broken, Mellia looked across the pond to see three dark figures enter the grove behind Sollix and Janus. Before the two wounded keepers could raise a fight, the figure in front sent a dark blue spiraling spellfiber, tightly binding the troll and the wizard. The dark magic covered their mouths, but Mellia saw from their faces that they were in great pain.

Takeji picked up a staff from the ground near his feet and began shooting bright white bullets in the direction of the approaching Darkentine poachers. One bullet blew past the figure in the front, singeing the midnight blue robes and knocking his hood back.

Victor Heatheros's pale face grimaced in the sunlight. Deep red scars lined his pale cheeks. Time slowed down for Mellia as she saw her sworn enemy. She barely noticed Kitsune dive into the bushes, running away from the melee. She heard the frantic flapping of papery wings as the cranes huddled behind Takeji, now too late for them to become invisible. She smelled a putrid scent of hatred and rot coming from the three figures.

The other two poachers stood over Janus and Sollix, taunting them and tightening the ropes. Hearing Janus's muffled cry brought Mellia back to real time. Heatheros began to dodge the old wizard's bullets and flick them out of the air, as though Takeji's ancient magic was a cloud of annoying gnats.

"Finally, the cranes," Victor purred triumphantly. "You hid them well last time, old man. But here we are."

Mellia stepped between Heatheros and Takeji. She felt her breath quicken, and she thought about herself back in Palenque, crying herself to sleep because she was grieving her mother. She wove a dark spell between her fingers and pushed it towards Heatheros.

The evil wizard laughed and attempted to push it away with his wand. Mellia's magic struck true, and Heatheros's smile faded, replaced with surprise. Pieces of Mellia's spellfiber had burned through his robes.

He glared at her menacingly. "Are you sure you don't want to join me, Child? Your magic matches mine," Heatheros said, sending black tendrils towards Takeji.

Mellia focused on a stronger Blazeguard, one that wasn't rooted in dark magic. She pictured her mother's smiling face and the way she knitted her brow when making herbal remedies. The Blazeguard faded from writhing black to the bright lilac color Mellia had practiced.

"Neathersby is an idiot sending children after this most precious resource," Victor declared.

He raised his wand and flung a dark spell towards Mellia, hitting her in the stomach. She felt the air leave her, and her body folded. Heatheros volleyed more magic that slashed at her arms and legs. Mellia tried to return fire, but she couldn't get a clear shot through Heatheros's rapid blasts.

Takeji slammed his staff into the ground, creating a shockwave that knocked Heatheros down. The evil poacher righted himself, creating a shield to block Takeji and Mellia's fire.

Suddenly, a large crash sounded through the trees where Sollix and Janus lay. One of the giant Komainu leapt into the glen, landing on top of the poachers and then batting them around with its giant paws. Sollix and Janus tried to maneuver away from the big cat, which was not an easy feat while bound with spellfiber.

"Woohoo!" A loud shriek came from atop the Komainu. The trio recognized Kitsune's gravelly battle cry. The lion now had one poacher in its mouth, throwing her into the air and catching her between its teeth. The poacher's hood fell off as she careened through the air, revealing the tell-tale green hue and pointed ears of a gobliness. The other poacher's robe had come off as the Komainu kicked it around under its hulking paw.

Kitsune pointed her wand towards Janus and Sollix, slicing through their magical bonds. She whispered something in her mount's ear, and the cat released the unconscious, soggy lady goblin next to her counterpart, a dirt-covered, robeless troll. Kitsune bound them up in her own orange spellfiber rope as Janus and Sollix stumbled to help Mellia.

Seeing his fellow hunters incapacitated fueled Victor Heatheros's anger further. Heatheros clapped his hands together, and a large black blast hit Takeji in the chest. The old man crumpled to the ground.

"I'm going to kill you next, gnelf. But maybe I will throw the old wizard here in the cage with your mother," he taunted.

Mellia's vision went black. She could feel Lifebender burning on her finger. She pointed it at Heatheros, willing him to die with all of her heart. The stone set in the ring glowed so brightly that Mellia thought it could be seen from the sky. Thick gray smoke poured from the stone and formed into a blurry humanoid figure.

The figure floated through the forcefield Heatheros had rapidly conjured. He backpedaled and tripped over a root, falling to the ground. The vaporous figure leapt onto Heatheros, placing its long blurry fingers on the poacher's throat. Heatheros held his hands up to push the being away, but they slipped through the ether. He conjured up a dark spell that passed through the creature and dissipated harmlessly into the air.

"Mellia, stop!" Sollix and Janus yelled, stumbling to her spot on the shore of the pond.

"No!" she screamed. "He's a killer, and he doesn't deserve to live."

Janus, Sollix, and Biko reached out for Mellia, who was still pointing the ring towards the poacher. His white face had turned reddish-purple. He flailed, too weak to cast any more spells. The smoky figure continued to grasp Heatheros's neck tightly. In seconds, the poacher's body went limp, and he no longer struggled. Mellia heard a dark voice from deep inside of her.

End him, the voice hissed angrily. Mellia thought of her mother, of Biko's family, of Kitsune's tribe. *Use the dagger,* it encouraged. She reached inside her robe, placing the diamond edge against his throat. *Tear his mind to pieces before you cut his throat,* the wrathful voice shrieked, almost gleefully.

She felt Biko's tiny hand on her shoulder. *Let him go,* the monkey whispered into her mind. *This is not the way; this is not you,* Biko begged. Mellia wanted to keep going. It felt good to see the limp wizard dying on the ground. Her ears roared, and her breath was shallow. Sweat soaked her body through her robes. She felt the calming plea of the Satori, who had experienced even greater loss at the hands of the poacher. Kitsune was yelling for her to stop, and she saw the stricken faces of Sollix and Janus by her side.

Mellia let go. She called back the Lifebender, and at her command it disappeared back into the stone as though it was never there. In unison, Kitsune, Janus, and Sollix summoned woven spell-fibers, covering the unconscious Heatheros and ensuring that the poacher would not move.

28

Mellia sagged to the ground. Tears poured down her face. She couldn't believe she had almost killed someone.

"Mellia, come here, Child." The rough, weakened voice of Takeji broke through her grief and shock. Her three companions kept their weapons pointed at the unconscious Heatheros. Takeji lay on the ground nearby. Heatheros's spell had burned through his robes, and Mellia could see internal bleeding under the old man's skin.

She knew the ancient wizard was dying. The child-like spark in his eyes was dimming rapidly, and suddenly he looked each of the hundreds of years of his age. He struggled to breathe and winced in pain each time he tried to inhale. Mellia grabbed his hand and his skin felt cold.

"Why didn't you help my mother?" she asked, begging the wizard for answers.

"Child, I am sorry for that. But your mother is still alive. It is your destiny to find her, but your journey of life holds so much more. You must follow the path of good, not evil, to find her. Swear this to me," he insisted, growing weaker with each word.

Mellia nodded, a silent promise. She waved her hands over

Takeji, willing Lifebender to save him. The ring's glow returned, a fierce bright white, rays glowing through the aged translucent webs of his fingers. Takeji placed his hand over hers.

"No, it is my time to leave this world," he whispered. Mellia could not speak; her throat closed with emotion. Her tears splashed on Takeji's face as the old man loosed his fingers from hers and weakly waved his hand.

Mellia saw a sparkling silver breeze float over the cranes. The chromatic wisps settled on the origami birds, and they dissipated peacefully into the air. Gone forever. Takeji managed a tight grin. "Don't worry, young gnelf. There are still cranes remaining." She looked around frantically for any sign of the majestic and angled birds.

Ignoring the cries and curses of the restrained poachers who witnessed the destruction of their coveted immortality spell, he motioned her close. He moved his lips and his words were almost imperceptible.

"There is something for you over there, under that bunch of reeds. I have chosen you to keep the cranes. You, my child, are loyal, fierce, humble, and smart. Just who I have been waiting for," the old man whispered. He limply raised his finger again, and the same silvery threads floated up and settled on Takeji. His lips relaxed into a peaceful smile, and his still body began to dissolve into a swirl of glittering filaments that climbed gracefully towards the sun.

Mellia took a moment to dry her tears. She pushed away her anger at Takeji and paused to think about the noble, ancient wizard who had given his life to ensure his creations did not fall into the wrong hands. When she was done, she headed over to the area Takeji had shown her. She pulled some stiff water bamboo stalks out of the way, and in a soft bed of tamped down reeds, cattails, and leaves lay three cream-colored paper eggs. Mellia stumbled back in shock, then jumped again when she heard a hissing noise.

Mellia quickly realized the hissing was magic. Kitsune had sent an emergency flare spell up into the sky, to summon Guild of Light Council Members. Immediately, Ironin Sahele, Jemima Bloomingdale, and Celora Ambrosia landed near the Komainu, who was lying on its side, licking its paws.

The Guild members landed with their wands out, ready to strike. Kitsune, Janus, and Sollix all began talking at once, recounting their adventure and their victorious battle. Edging away from the nest, Mellia joined the group. With barely a glance, Celora waved her wand towards Sollix's and Janus's jade-encrusted wounds. White light closed the wounds, and the infecting jade crystals fell harmlessly to the ground.

Ironin interrupted in his deep voice, "One at a time. You will all get a turn sharing your heroics today. I'm so proud of you all."

Ironin, Jemima, and Celora prepared the three poachers for transport, wrapping them with an infinitely stronger Blazeguard spell.

"What happens to them now?" Mellia asked. "They know where my mother is," she said, raising her chin towards Ironin.

"They go to the Madstone Asylum in Tibet. We will get your mother's location out of them by any means necessary and then send in a rescue team," Ironin promised. "Thanks to you," he added, gazing at Mellia with what she thought was pride. Kitsune began to walk away, motioning for the Komainu to follow her.

"Kitsune!" Ironin bellowed. "Stop right there."

The fox woman turned, looking startled. Ironin continued in a gentler tone, "It is clear to me that you are a Yokai that changes sides. You should not have abandoned Admiral and Chief Medic Kelgwyn in their time of need. However, you have gone above and beyond to ensure the safety of these promising young ones. I would like to offer you a position as a covert operator with the Guild."

Mellia, Janus, and Sollix looked eagerly at their new friend.

"You have nothing left here," Sollix said. "The cranes are gone, Kitsune. You'll be lonely here. Even with those horrible giant cats to keep you company." Kitsune rubbed her chin, pretending to consider the offer. The Komainu hissed at Sollix, running his rough tongue over jade teeth.

"I'm in," Kitsune said happily. "On to the next adventure."

"Are you ready to spellaport back? I can send you right to the Great Banquet Hall at the Preserve," Jemima Bloomingdale asked.

Mellia gave her roommates a heavy gaze and shook her head. She was thinking of the nest and Takeji's dying wish. She wasn't sure why, but she did not want to share the cranes with anyone but her friends for a while.

"I think we will go back the way we came, with Adeline," Mellia said, shooting a heavy glance towards her friends. Biko groaned. Sollix looked at her quizzically but did not protest. Janus elbowed him, understanding his friend's weighted gaze.

29

When the Guild members had left the glen, escorting the angry poachers to Madstone, Mellia motioned to her friends. They walked over to the bunch of reeds Takeji had indicated before he passed. Mellia pointed at the nest.

"Takeji gave you his cranes--and the secret to immortality..." Janus murmured. Staring in awe at the tiny eggs, Mellia realized the weight of her new responsibility. She gently picked up the entire nest and tucked it and the eggs into her robe pocket. Biko gingerly slid into Mellia's pocket and wrapped himself around the eggs like a mother hen.

Before leaving the grove, the keepers made a small stone pile in honor of Takeji. Mellia plucked a few of the deep pink lotus flowers from the pond and created a circle around the stone effigy.

The trip back to the island shore was uneventful. Mellia was silent, lost in her thoughts. She thought of her father, wondering if she had been too harsh on him. The map seemed relieved to be reunited with Sollix, and unrolled gently in his hands. A magical green line appeared, cutting a straight and true path down the mountain, only veering off to small creeks to refill StreamDeep.

When they reached the edge of the tree line, the group squinted, looking for their boat. The sun reflected off the ocean and blinded the trio, who were used to dark dankness of the jungle. Adeline, the boat, was there. She was half submerged in the water. Mellia's eyes bulged looking at the fist-sized hole in the middle of the boat.

"Ugh...we're sunk," Janus moaned, looking at the broken vessel. The three sat down dejectedly on the beach. The map leapt out of the bag and fell to the ground, inching across the white sand like some kind of parchment worm. Sollix picked it up, mumbling.

"That was a bit dramatic, Map."

When he unrolled the scroll, he saw a bright red line leading down the beach. Unsure what it meant, the group followed the line for about a mile. They moved slowly, adrenaline having worn off.

Seemingly out of nowhere, a small thatch hut appeared. Shrugging his shoulders, Sollix declared, "Well, we might as well go in. Nothing to lose. Maybe we can find something to plug the Adeline's giant hole!"

The one room shack was covered in dust. Glass jars filled with coral and driftwood tied with fishing line hung from the walls. An old blackened kettle and dented pan sat over a fire pit filled with burned wood and large stones. In the corner a dingy nest of blankets was piled in the corner, along with stretched animal skins in bone frames.

With surprising care and exquisite technique, Kitsune had drawn charcoal scenes of Yokai fishing, climbing coconut trees, laughing, and playing games. Mellia pocketed a small drawing of Takeji dancing with the Yokai. Mellia could feel the loneliness emanating from the pictures, and her dark anger reemerged. For the hundredth time on her journey she thought, *the Darkentine have taken so much.*

"I've got it!" Janus exclaimed, hovering over a large glass jug. It was filled with muddy, bubbly liquid contained by a large rubber stopper. He yanked with all of his strength, but the cork stayed fixed. Sollix stretched his arms, cracking his knuckles out in front of him. "Move aside, my friend."

He yanked the rubber stopper, pulling it free. The bubbling concoction, which smelled like rancid coconut beer, sprayed out from the tight pressure of the jug. Some of the rank foam landed on Janus's blood, dirt, and sweat stained hanfu. The silken dragons made gagging sounds. Their eyes bulged.

"Last straw!" Janus shouted, grabbing the rubber cork and stomping back to the Adeline. Mellia and Sollix followed behind, giggling silently at the angry Gaiden.

Using all of his strength, Sollix pulled the water-filled boat from the water. Janus shoved the cork into the hole, stopping incoming water. Tipping the boat to fully drain it, Sollix hummed "Frere Jacques." Now floating on top of the water, the Adeline swayed in the tide, unmoving. Sollix motioned to Mellia and Janus, and they managed to hum along, singing some parts of the chorus.

Suddenly, the Adeline burst to life. She sailed back and forth excitedly just off shore, waving her sails high in the air. Sollix whistled through his teeth, and the weary adventurers boarded and sat down heavily in the boat.

Mellia could hear Biko mumbling complaints in Satori, preparing for the queasiness of ocean travel.

Biko had taken to sitting with the tiny knot of eggs that Mellia was guarding in her upper coat pocket. Mellia wrapped her coat tightly around her, sharing her body heat with Biko and the eggs. Adeline set off efficiently, cutting through the waves of the shoreline without pause. Sollix wrapped himself up in his robes and fell asleep.

Mellia didn't even flinch when the behemoth head of the infant Ikuchi surfaced in the water. Biko abandoned the eggs to greet the young sea snake. Biko managed to ascertain that its name was Ichinomaya, and his mother was Mirimaya.

The giant creature dove under Adeline and pushed the boat towards home. Feeling safe with the Ikuchi and Adeline at the helm, Janus and Mellia closed their eyes to sleep.

Mellia felt the familiar chill of Scottish air slipping through her cloak and chilling her core. She opened her eyes to the foggy beach of the lake shore and the verdant greens of the forested wall.

"Home!" Sollix shouted, jumping from the boat.

Before he ran towards the castle grounds, he murmured something sweet and quiet in French to Adeline, and she reared her bow up in the air. Janus managed to stay on their feet. Mellia was flung from the boat, but Ichinomaya caught her in mid-air with his tail and set her down on the shore. This time Mellia didn't mind getting the fishy oil on her robes.

She placed her hand on the sea monster. She stroked his head and sent waves of gratitude into the mind of the docile Ikuchi. Nessie and Ichinomaya flicked tails, splashing at each other. The creature eventually turned to leave, disappearing under the inky waters of the Loch. Adeline sailed away to a dock in a mysterious location.

"First bath!" Janus shouted and spellaported to their shared living quarters. Sollix skipped to reach the stone hallways of the dorm.

Mellia was relieved to be back, but she didn't feel as relieved as her friends. She knew that she needed to reach out to her father, and she knew she needed to find her mother. Fueled with a new purpose, Mellia leapt through the air, catching Sollix.

"Second bath," Mellia said, laughing. "On second thought, you are one smelly troll. You can go first."

When they arrived at the room, Janus looked impeccable. Their hair was back to its normal silken sheen, and they had a red fresh robe with golden dragons that undulated across the back and sleeves. Their skin was fresh and moisturized with a healthy glow.

30

Mellia placed the nest on her dresser, and Biko curled around it, keeping the eggs warm. Sollix reached to touch one, but Biko swiped his hand away.

"Biko's become pretty attached," explained Mellia.

"I don't blame him; they literally hold the secrets to immortality," Janus said.

After cleaning the filth of their first mission, Mellia, Janus, and Sollix headed to the great hall for dinner. As they pushed open the heavy wooden door, the hall grew silent, devoid of its usual mealtime chatter. Mellia felt flushed as the beings stared at her. She saw Enna's jaw drop, a fork full of potatoes frozen half way to her delicate pixie mouth.

Biko climbed up to Mellia's shoulder, flexing his thin monkey arms and showing off for the crowd. Suddenly, the keepers burst into a cheer.

A boisterous bunch of trolls scrummed around Sollix, patting him roughly on the back and asking how many poachers he helped to capture. Mellia laughed as Sollix took credit for Kitsune's clever magic. She saw Sollix trying to shake off his cousins and reach Jaya, who sat at the back of the dining hall.

The pixies fawned over Janus. They touched their arm seductively, much to the chagrin of the dragons on his robe. They batted their white blond eyelashes and pretended to hang on their every word.

Mellia sat alone at her usual spot at the table. She focused on her plate of buttery, smooth mashed potatoes, grateful for having plentiful amounts of food.

A lithe figure with bowed legs strode into the dining room. Her wizard's hat was tipped over her eyes. *Feign,* Mellia thought, feeling as though a swarm of bees were trying to escape from inside her stomach.

Her heart began to pound so loudly, Mellia wondered if anyone else could hear it. As though the keeper could feel Mellia's stare, she turned to look at the gawking gnelf. Feign tipped her hat towards Mellia and offered her a small smile.

Out of nowhere, a looming figure blocked Mellia's view of the shapeshifter. Instinctively reaching for her wand, Mellia paused, seeing the rough brown fabric of Neathersby's suit. Mellia looked up at the cyclops with a new confidence.

"Back, I see," Neathersby said with a proud grin. "I'm proud of you, girl. Fret and I had bets on if you would make it. I'm not going to say which one of us placed our coin in your favor," she said, laughing.

"Well, I hope you won," Mellia said dully, not appreciating the humor at her expense.

"Child, I am trying to make a joke. I am rarely impressed. However, you and your friends prevented the poachers from obtaining the cranes, recruited a new covert operator, captured the most notorious Darkentine wizard, and befriended an Ikuchi," Neathersby added.

"I'm ready to find my mother. I have proved myself," Mellia countered, ignoring Neathersby's accolades.

"Come with me," Neathersby commanded, already back to business. She pulled her wand from her suit, and Mellia found herself spellaported into Neathersby's office at the top of the turret. Once her dizziness subsided, Mellia saw Kitsune. She smiled and ran over to hug the fox woman, who embraced her tightly in return. Sollix and Janus stood smiling next to Kitsune.

"You three," Jonathan intoned in what Mellia called his "admiral voice." He stepped from behind the desk, and Neathersby, Fret, and Kitsune reflexively stood at attention under his deep and commanding tones. "You have proven yourselves to be brave, loyal, and strong. What's more, you ensured that the Darkentine poachers did not escape with the origami cranes."

The admiral pulled four gold star-shaped medals from his pocket. He nodded at Kitsune.

"Thank you for keeping our three keepers safe," he said, attaching the medal to the chest of her new white gee. "You have risked the wrath of the Darkentine Council, but you have earned the protection and fealty of the Guild of Light."

The admiral reached towards Janus with one of the pins outstretched, and Janus merely held their hand out. They did not like their robes being touched or poked with pins, even if they were medals of honor. The admiral attached the third badge to Sollix's robe, and Sollix stood even straighter, grinning madly from ear to ear.

When he reached Mellia, the admiral stuck his hand out awkwardly. At the same time, Mellia leaned in to hug her father. The two were caught in an awkward dance, which ended in Jonathan simply pinning the medal to his daughter's robe.

"Mellia, I'm very sorry I was so hard on you. Without your mother to guide me, I am afraid I'm not the most skilled father. I was afraid that if I was too easy on you, you would not learn what you needed to live through such a perilous undertaking," he explained.

Before Mellia could respond, Sollix interjected, "Yeah, you were a bit of a mossback."

The admiral stood up to his full height, and glared at Sollix, danger in his eyes.

"You were a bit of a mossback…Sir…wait. I just meant…" Sollix stuttered, terrified. The admiral raised his fist, and Sollix squeezed his eyes shut. The admiral brushed the end of the troll's nose and made a "boop" sound.

"There's your one freebie, Troll. Call me anything except Sir, and I'll tie you up in a Blazeguard and take you to Madstone myself," the admiral said, grinning widely. He did not seem to notice that Mellia hadn't responded.

The group of keepers and warriors talked late into the night. The admiral listened as Mellia recounted how Takeji and the cranes had disappeared. Mellia inched closer and closer to her father until eventually they touched shoulders.

She talked about how brave Janus and Sollix had been fighting the hypnotized Ikuchi sea monster. Fret appeared with tea and freshened everyone's mugs. After midnight, Neathersby began to yawn.

"Well, Jonathan, get to it then," she said, elbowing him in the way of old friends.

"Thanks to the...let's say...*persuasive* methods of the goblins holding the poachers you captured, we were able to get information about your mother."

Mellia felt her breath go shallow with anticipation. She couldn't believe she had her father back, and now she could reunite her whole family.

Neathersby scanned the room, resting her eyes on Mellia, and asked, "Are you ready for your next mission? You're going to need a warmer coat."

THE END

ABOUT THE AUTHOR

Amanda Marisol lives in the beautiful Bay Area of California, with her two firecracker daughters, her partner, nicknamed Brioche, and two alarmingly bossy dogs. When she is not writing, she teaches third and fourth grade, and moonlights as a lecturer for a local University. You can find her hiking the back trails of Sycamore Grove or in her front yard, trying desperately to learn the art of bonsai.

Learn more about Preserve of Enchanted Creatures, Amanda's next book, and Preserve Keepers on her Web site -
www.amandamarisol.com

ACKNOWLEDGMENTS

To you, the reader! Yes you. Thank you for reading my tale, I hope you enjoyed. As an Indie author, our bread and butter is reviews! Drop your thoughts on the story on Amazon or Goodreads.

Heather Rubert for patiently reading terrible draft after draft, and sticking with me throughout. "Maybe someday she will understand dialogue tags," Heather wondered with a smile.

Candice Broersma for bringing all of these characters to life. You lending your brilliant artistry sparked a fire in me to complete this project.

Adrienne Patino-Dunn, for lending your talents as a narrator, and adding dimension to the audiobook. You are brilliant!

Brian Werner for patiently allowing me to explore the characters and plot over brunch after brunch.

Ellen Yeoman for being curious enough to keep me going.

Darren Wong for showing excitement for this project, and being willing to share your honest opinion. Don't ever lose that skill.

Eli Sugar for your cover opinions, and calling me my pen name in public. You're one of my favorite kids, and your enthusiasm kept me going.

Luna and Jayden keep sparkling.

Grandma Norma for always being proud of me.

Eric Yeomans Three, Four, Five and Six, Linda Yeoman, Heather, Lochlan and Julian, thank you for believing in this nut!

Lara Foland, Lia Vittori, Rita and Fredo Bhakta Mathew – thank you for being my truest lifelong friends, for always being there, and supporting me through thick and thin

DUCHESS WIZARDRESS OF NEWCASTLE MARGARET CAVENDISH'S ABRIDGED FIELD GUIDE

Abridged Field Guide to Enchanted Creatures, Magical Plants, and Proven Spells

Greetings, fellow adventurers and seekers of knowledge! I am Duchess Wizard Margaret Cavendish, a philosopher, poet, and lover of all things magical. As you embark on your journey through the mystical world of spells and enchanted creatures, allow me to be your guide. There is always a bit of truth to all the folklore we read, and here's what I have discovered in my travels and research into the magical sciences.

Magic spells are powerful tools that can be used to alter reality and bend the laws of nature to your will. From simple incantations to complex rituals, spells have been used for centuries to heal the sick, protect the vulnerable, and even summon otherworldly beings.

But be warned, dear reader, for not all creatures that inhabit the realm of magic are friendly. Enchanted creatures, from mischievous fairies to fearsome dragons, can be both wondrous and dangerous. It is important to know how to approach them with caution and respect, lest you find yourself in a perilous situation.

In this field guide, we will explore the various types of magic spells and enchanted creatures you may encounter on your adventures. We will delve into the history and lore of each, as well as provide practical advice on how to interact with them safely and effectively.

So ready your wand, sharpen your senses, and let us journey forth into the enchanted realm of magic and wonder!

Amikiri - This dangerous, malevolent creature is the bane of all fishermen near and far. Part snake, part crow, part lobster, this three-foot-long beast tears through the most magic of nets. Ancient relative of the Ikuchi sea monster. Hunted for their magical gills, which allow the holder to breathe both air and water.

Baku - Don't let these cute, tapir-looking fellows fool you. They have the telepathic power to put you to sleep and read your dreams. Using their long nose, they can devour your dreams if they are angry, or your nightmares if they consider you a friend. Used for dangerous psychic dream reading by the Darkentine Guild.

Chimera – These serpentine creatures have the ability to breathe fire. They are untrainable. Grecian Chimera have a lion's head, a goat's body, and a dragon's tail. They enjoy fingertips and breathing fire at each other.

Elegons- Very large and very aggressive, Elegons are carnivorous, with sharp teeth, clawed wings, and a scaled whipping tail. They have the large legs and trunks of an elephant, and often bludgeon their prey with their large feet. Though they have colorful wings, their flight is clumsy due to their weight. They enjoy basking in the warm sun and being ridden by trolls during long rugby games.

Equidae - A cross between a deer and a horse, the Equidae make their home in arid plains, deserts, and mountain foothills. They are extremely fast, and many have been tamed for transportation purposes. Equidae love to eat sagebrush and are known to consume the occasional tumbleweed.

Elf - Elves are folkloric magical beings that originated in Germany. For the purposes of this story, elves are very powerful sorcerers, and tend to be leaders in both good and evil in the magical world.

Gauze - An ancient magical barrier created when humankind began to embrace religion and vilify magic and enchanted creatures. To prevent war with the humans, the wizards and sorcerers at the time created an invisible blockade made from magical filaments. When someone hits the Gauze, they simply move away from it, unaware that it's even there.

Gnome - English creatures, emerging during the Renaissance period, gnomes are smaller than humans and like to be closer to the earth. They have extraordinary healing powers and a natural acumen for using plants to create curative potions.

Goblin - Lore of the goblin originated in the European Middle Ages. They are known to be full of mischief, and are characterized by their green pallor and pointed ears.

Guardgoyle - Originally a standard part of French architecture, Guardgoyles are a species of gargoyle that have been highly trained to guard important buildings and places of magic. They have extraordinary hearing and are very loyal.

Ikuchi - The Ikuchi are Japanese sea snakes. They are dangerous and giant undersea predators. They produce a thick oil that sits on the top of the water. They are valued by the Darkentine Council because they are apex hunters and swim quickly through the water. Ideal for sea battles.

Stinging Lacewings - Deadly winged creatures that draw beings in with their ethereally beautiful lacelike wings. One sting from these creatures, and you become slave to the next person who commands you, until you die three days later.

Komainu - Catlike creatures, usually found in pairs, with roots from many areas of Asia. This animal has a mustache and wide eyes, with sharp jade claws and teeth that are ideal for guarding. Formerly statues, the Komainu were brought to life by Takeji when he sensed threats to the paper cranes.

Owltender- Owltenders are a specific race of wizards that have created a symbiotic relationship with owls. They are highly intelligent and often devise spells. The Owltenders have been around for hundreds of years and curate the global history of magical beings.

Pixie - Pixies are a lot like fairies. Stories about pixies began in early thirteenth century Britain. They have evolved to be humanoid, white-haired beauties, with strong magic and a mean streak.

Saemarnir (Sammie) - These piglike creatures sustain the keepers at the zoo. The legend says they are killed each night and cooked by a God. The creature's spirit goes to Valhalla, where they are fed rich and enchanted grass from a heavenly meadow before reincarnating each day to be food for magical creatures all over again.

Shapeshifter - The shapeshifter race is ancient, perhaps predating humanity. In fact, some say many humans are shapeshifters that became trapped in their human form.

Skvader - Emerging from Sweden, these winged rodents are larger than bears and are both friendly and mischievous.

Steelwood - A particularly strong magical wood used by most magical beings. Steelwood trees are extremely hard wood with steel twisted through. Steelwood trees are grown over the metal mines of dwarves and are carved with diamond tools.

Troll - Trolls are large, hulking beings with significant strength. They are extremely family oriented and live in large tribal communities around the world. The largest groups are in Africa. Trolls are hunters, and can overpower most large magical creatures.

Ukiuk Dwarves – These cold-weather dwarves have the power of "beaming," which is to magically travel within different shafts of light in the same area. They have a symbiotic relationship with the Yeti clan that coexist in their arctic home.

Uniceros - Famous for their silver mucous skin excretions, uniceros are a rare and hunted species. Their oil can heal even the gravest of wounds. They are highly prized by Darkentine Poachers.

Yeti - A creature that inhabits Nepal, Tibet, and other cold areas. It is ape-like and covered in white fur. Coveted for their enchanted fur that can warm any object, Yeti hide from most beings. They coexist with the Ukiuk dwarf tribe.

Yokai - These supernatural beings, on the island of Oshima, are half fox and half human, and they are generally immortal. They have a pearl tied to their tail by magic thread, a feature that is tied to their immortality.

Image - author credit and enhanced with AI